P9-DBK-291

SNOW JOB

ALSO BY CHARLES BENOIT

YOU

FALL FROM GRACE

COLD CALLS

FOR ADULTS

RELATIVE DANGER

OUT OF ORDER

NOBLE LIES

CHARLES BENOIT

SNOW

WITHDRAWN
LORETTE WILMOT LIBRARY
NAZARETH COLLEGE

CLARION BOOKS
Houghton Mifflin Harcourt
BOSTON NEW YORK

CLARION BOOKS

3 Park Avenue, New York,
New York 10016

Copyright © 2016
by Charles Benoit

All rights reserved. For information about permission to reproduce selections from this book, write to trade.permissions@hmhco.com or to Permissions, Houghton Mifflin Harcourt Publishing Company, 3 Park Avenue, 19th Floor, New York, New York 10003.

Clarion Books is an imprint of Houghton Mifflin Harcourt Publishing Company.

WWW.HMHCO.COM

The text was set in Figural Std.
Art by Richard Mia
Book design by Sharismar Rodriguez

Library of Congress Cataloging in Publication Data

Names: Benoit, Charles. » Title: Snow job / Charles Benoit.
Description: Boston ; New York : Clarion Books, Houghton Mifflin Harcourt, [2016] » Summary: "Nick has created the perfect list of rules for remaking his life. But meeting dark-eyed Dawn, hanging out with teen thug Zod, and making illegal deliveries are nowhere on that list. Small steps lead to an avalanche of consequences as one boy attempts to take charge of his destiny." —Provided by publisher. » Identifiers: LCCN 2015020440 | ISBN 9780544318861 (hardback) Subjects: | CYAC: Conduct of life—Fiction. | Interpersonal relations—Fiction. | Drug traffic—Fiction. | BISAC: JUVENILE FICTION / Action & Adventure / General. | JUVENILE FICTION / Law & Crime. | JUVENILE FICTION / Boys & Men.
Classification: LCC PZ7.B447114 Sn 2016 | DDC [Fic]—dc23
LC record available at http://lccn.loc.gov/2015020440

Manufactured in the United States of America
DOC 10 9 8 7 6 5 4 3 2 1
4500576810

ROSE:
WE CAN HITCH A RIDE TO ROCKAWAY BEACH.

J F
Ben

SPECIAL THANKS TO THE RAMONES FOR RESCUING ME.
AND TO JOAN JETT FOR SETTING THE BAR SO HIGH.
— C.B.

1977

I rounded the corner and headed to the cafeteria.

Now if I was *really* following the list, I'd have gone to an art gallery or a pool hall or down to the lake to watch the waves roll in — any place different from where I usually went. But I was already at school and I didn't have a car and it was really cold that morning. Other than the library or the smoking lounge, there wasn't anywhere to go. It was second lunch, and the cafeteria was where the bangers would be. For reasons known only to the office gods, I had third lunch, and that meant I'd been spending a lot less of my day hanging out with the bangers and more time alone. And that meant more time thinking about all the things in my life that needed to change. Like me.

I walked into the cafeteria and headed for the back of the room.

Bangerstan.

Dan-O was suspended and Vicki never came to school on a Friday, but most of the regulars were there, with Tony — empty quart of Mountain Dew bouncing in his hands — doing the talking. As usual. For a moment I was tempted to turn around and go back to class, but old habits die hard. And — I'll admit it — I wanted a reaction.

They didn't disappoint.

I leaned a chair against the wall and balanced back and waited. It took a second or two for it to sink in, then Tony pointed at me and said, "What the hell you got on?"

I glanced down at my ensemble, then looked back at Tony. "It's called a shirt and tie."

"No shit, Sherlock. Why you wearing it? You lose a bet?" That made OP laugh, but OP laughed at anything Tony said, so it didn't count.

Jay looked up from the science homework he was copying. "He looks like an asshole."

"Or a narc," Tony said. "Nerds don't even dress like that. What's the matter, Mommy forget to wash your real clothes?"

"Check out his stupid sneakers," OP said, laughing, of course. To make it easy for them, I swung a foot up onto the table, dropping it down with a thud.

A new pair of white Chuck Taylor All-Stars, colored in, checkerboard style, with a marker.

A green marker.

While they stared at the sneaker, I looked around the table. Nothing but flannels and band T-shirts, every guy a slight variation of the last, the Levi's and work boots as interchangeable as the shaggy haircuts. That made me smile. My journey had begun.

"You're an idiot," Tony said.

I let the smile roll into a smirk. It was a small gesture, easy to miss if you weren't paying attention. But Tony was, and I knew that my smirk had pissed him off. I swung my foot back down. Mission accomplished.

But Tony couldn't let it drop and had to say something. I assumed it would be more about my clothes — they hadn't even noticed the haircut — but he surprised me and said, "You don't know shit about football."

That wasn't true.

I knew how the game was played, I knew the names of the NFL teams or at least the cities they played for, I knew some of the current players and some of the legends, and living where we did in New York State — a thirty-minute bike ride from Lake Ontario and an hour by car from Niagara Falls — I knew enough about the Buffalo Bills to not sound completely ignorant. Tony was wrong, I did *know* shit about football.

I just didn't *give* a shit about football.

"Check this out," Tony said, backhanding the sleeve of the Roach's smoke-saturated jean jacket. "Nick thinks the Bills are going to beat the Jets this week."

The Roach looked at Tony, then at me, then back at Tony. "Bill who?"

"The *Buffalo* Bills, dickhead. Nick thinks they're actually gonna beat the New York Jets."

The Roach said nothing but kept his red-rimmed eyes on Tony.

"It's football," Jay said without looking up. "He's talking about football."

"Oh, right," the Roach said, the two words taking forever to fall out.

"And Nick here"— Tony pointing at me in case the Roach had forgotten who they were talking about—"thinks the *Bills* are gonna win."

No, I didn't. It was just something I had said when I was at my locker that morning. Mrs. Grant had been standing by her classroom door, five feet away, picking *that* morning to be all chatty. Maybe it was the tie. She asked me how my grades were, how I was doing in social studies, asking if I was looking at colleges, me with nothing to say, keeping it to one-word answers. Then she asked who I thought would win that weekend, the Bills or the Jets—as if she could care what I thought—but I didn't want to be a jerk, so I said I thought the Bills would win. Then she started laughing like it was the stupidest thing she'd heard a kid say in her thirty years as a teacher, shouting across the hall to Mr. Cermak, "Nick thinks the Bills are gonna beat the Jets," and everybody getting a good laugh at that.

Here's the thing: Tony didn't care about football. None of us bangers did. It was part of being a banger. But Tony wasn't going to pass up a free shot at me.

"The Bills are gonna get crushed. The only one who'd be stupid enough to think they had a chance would be some dweeb with his head up his ass and shit for brains." Now it was Tony's turn to smirk. "Like Nick."

I knew that if I said nothing, Tony would move on, and the random, offhand comment I had said just to say something would be forgotten. But I had my list now, and backing down wasn't on it. So, despite my not giving a shit, I said, "Wanna bet?"

Tony looked at me and laughed, then he hit the Roach's arm again. "Did you hear that?"

"Hear what?"

"Numbnuts here wants to know if I want to bet."

The Roach blinked. "Are you still talking about football?"

"All right," Tony said, "you're on." Then, after a pause, "Twenty bucks."

I had two dollars crumpled up in the front pocket of my jeans, a quarter in that little pocket on the right side, and nine dollars at home, most of it in change. I earned a little bit above minimum wage—$2.65 an hour—and worked fourteen hours a week, usually less. It would take my whole paycheck to cover the bet. I didn't have money to be throwing away like that. But I did have my list, and the list had the answer.

I paused a second like I was weighing the odds, then I said, "Make it a hundred."

Jay looked up from someone else's paper. "For real?"

"Yeah," I said, and I could feel my leg start to shake. "Hundred bucks says the Bills beat the Browns this week."

"They're playing the frickin' Jets, you idiot."

Oh. I shrugged. "A hundred bucks."

They were all looking at Tony now—Jay, the Roach, Lou,

OP, Geralyn, Cici, stray kids at other tables close enough to hear. A hundred bucks? None of them had that kind of money. It was insane. I knew it, and I was sure that Tony knew it too.

"The bet's twenty," Tony said, disappointing everybody but me. "Take it or leave it."

So I took it, and that Sunday, the Buffalo Bills beat the New York Jets for their third and final win of the 1977 season.

THURSDAY, DECEMBER 15

KARLA TWISTED HER LIP AND BLEW THE CIGARETTE SMOKE straight up out of the corner of her mouth. I loved how she looked when she did that, tough, but considerate enough not to blow the smoke in your face. It made her look as old as her fake ID said she was. We were sitting on the back bumper of somebody's pickup truck behind the Pizza Hut where Karla waited tables. It was sunny and warm for mid-December, weeks since the last decent snowstorm, but there was still too much snow piled up to sit on the guardrail, our usual spot. And to get this straight right from the start, we weren't going out and we'd never fooled around, not even a little. We'd joke about it, each of us trying to out-crude the other, but that's as far as it ever went, which is good, since it would have just screwed it up.

"Tony pay you?"

"Not yet," I said.

"Think he will?"

"No. He's hoping I forget."

"Will you?"

"Probably."

"He'd make you pay if he won," she said.

"That's him."

She took a long drag on her Newport. "That bet thing? That wasn't because of your list, was it?"

It was, but I didn't admit it.

"And the scalp job?" She smiled and ran a finger over the top of my ear, the first time since sixth grade that it hadn't been hidden under my hair. It wasn't a brush cut or anything, but it was short. Most of the teachers had longer hair. "That part of it too?"

Right again, but I said, "Maybe."

"It's cute. But a list isn't going to change who you are. Life doesn't work like that."

"Why not?"

"Because you can't. It's not that simple."

I watched the smoke curl off the end of the cigarette and thought about my list. Four lines, eight words total. Seemed pretty simple to me. And so far it was working. People were talking about the bet. Girls I didn't know said they liked my haircut. I was still wearing the tie. Small stuff, yeah, but a start.

Another drag. "I can see shutting up Tony, that makes sense. But a hundred bucks on a football game?"

"Easy come, easy go," I said, like I had bags of cash under my bed.

She looked at me, then did that thing again with her lip and blew. "You're not that stupid."

"You'd be surprised at how stupid I can be."

"No, I wouldn't."

The back door of the Pizza Hut popped open. A guy in his twenties—mustache, red and white checkered shirt, clipboard—looked over at Karla. He made a production about staring at his watch, pushing the tiny button on the side, making sure we could see that it wasn't just some old-fashioned timepiece with hands but a shiny new Texas Instruments digital watch. He held the man-from-the-future pose way too long, then pulled the door closed.

"That was hardly fifteen minutes," Karla said, flicking the butt into a dirty snowbank as she stood. "Apparently all the regulars are at Jay's tomorrow. You gonna go?"

Hanging out at Jay's house was one of the reasons I'd made a list. "I wasn't planning on it."

"You got something else to do?"

"Not yet."

"There's no way I'm gonna spend another Friday night sitting around listening to the same scratchy side of the same Zeppelin album. Just meet me there. We'll figure something out."

I was looking forward to not going to Jay's at all, but it was Karla, so I'd be there. In a way, that was on the list too.

I stood up and brushed the road salt off my jeans. Giving up rock-star tees for a shirt and tie was one thing, but there was no way I was switching from jeans. I was walking her to the back door of the Pizza Hut when she said, all casual, "I heard Zod was asking about you today."

I stopped and, for a few beats, so did my heart. I put my hands in my pockets and looked past Karla, out through the parking lot, over the main road, and all the way back to middle school.

"It was years ago," Karla said. "Maybe he's over it."

I smiled at that.

"I'm sure it's nothing," she said.

"You're probably right," I said, knowing she was wrong.

Karla kicked the toe of her boot twice against the back door, and a busboy younger than me opened it. She ignored the kid's dopey smile, and before she went in, she looked at me. She started to say something, stumbled on the first word, turned, and went inside, pulling the steel door shut behind her.

FRIDAY, DECEMBER 16

THE STOP-N-GO WAS IN A PLAZA AT AN INTERSECTION A mile from my school. There was a narrow liquor store on one side of the Stop-N-Go, a dry cleaner on the other, and, next to that, a tiny office for an insurance agent. A tall wooden fence separated the twenty-car parking lot from the suburban houses in the neighborhood. Across the street was a funeral home, and there were competing gas stations on the other two corners.

Back when I was in middle school, cars would be lined up out into the street, waiting to buy gas, the price going up every day and "Out of Gas" signs posted every week. That was 1973. Now both stations sold gas for sixty cents, and there was never a line. The Roach used to pump gas at one of them, Vicki's cousin got a year's probation for stealing tires from the other.

I didn't mean to get a job at the Stop-N-Go — it just sorta happened. I had gone in for an application, part of a careers assignment in health class last year, and the next thing the store manager's asking if I can start on Saturday. So I stocked shelves and loaded the cooler and swept the parking lot and rang up customers — everything the manager didn't want to do, and all for $2.65 an hour. The job earned me some spending money, but it brought an end to my whopping five-dollars-a-week allowance.

Friday night at seven, I was at the register, the easiest job in the place.

Jay came in, looked around. "He here?"

"In the back," I said. "On the phone or something."

"Outstanding," Jay said, waving in Gordie, who sat behind the wheel of his rusted-out Maverick. "How much can we get for twenty-four bucks?"

I ran the numbers in my head, one of the few talents I had. "Two and a half cases of Bud. Or three of Miller."

"That's not enough. Can't you give a discount?"

"I'm not supposed to sell it to you at all." I nodded at Gordie as he came through the door. "Black Label's on sale," I said. "Six-pack for a buck and change. Cans. That's four and a half cases. Plus tax."

"Ugh. That's crap beer."

"It's better than no beer," Gordie said. He might have been flunking every class at school, but Gordie had plenty of common sense, which was uncommon for a banger.

I followed their reflections in the round mirror above the magazine rack as they walked to the coolers, watching to make sure they didn't lift a pack of Twinkies on their way down the bread aisle or chug a Miller pony while they looked in the cooler.

It was the running joke with the bangers that I had never stolen a thing from the store. Not so much as a pack of gum. I wasn't afraid of getting caught, and it had nothing to do with it being against the law — I just didn't do it and that was it. You don't need a list to tell you that stealing is wrong, but I thought it was cool how that one thing I knew was true fit with the four things I eventually wrote down. The stupid part of my attitude — to the bangers, anyway — is that I wouldn't let *them* steal anything. They could empty the place out when I wasn't working, but I made it clear that if they tried it when I was there, I'd turn them in. They didn't like it, but they never tested me on it, either.

Jay and Gordie were at the counter with two cases and a six-pack each when George came out of the back room.

I gave George an I've-got-this nod, then said to Jay, "Gotta proof you."

"Proof? You know I don't have —"

"Here," Gordie said, reaching around Jay to hand me his driver's license.

I made a good show of examining the card, reading both sides and double-checking the birth date.

August 12, 1960. Seventeen years old, and eight months away from the drinking age.

"Thanks," I said, handing the card back. "That'll be twenty-two eighty-two. Want any ice with that?"

Gordie gave me a half grin. "For free, right?"

I shook my head.

"That's bogus, dude," Gordie said, scooping the change up off the counter.

Jay picked up his half of the beer. "You coming over later?"

I shrugged. "Afraid so."

Ten minutes later, a light blue Trans Am pulled in fast to the parking lot, stopping with a screech in the lone handicap spot. The doors flung open and the *thumpa-thumpa, thumpa-thumpa* disco baseline shook the store windows.

Polys.

I knew the passenger, Frank Camden, a senior at Hently and, like every guy at the east-side private school, a total dick. He was wearing a gray and red silk shirt, unbuttoned down to the middle of his bony chest, and a pair of white polyester flares with a two-inch-wide red belt. His shoulder-length hair was parted in the middle, blow-dried to perfection, the feathered waves frozen in place by a half a can of hairspray. Around his neck he wore a strand of puka shells that had a turquoise stone the size of a quarter in the middle. His platform shoes put him over six feet, making him look even thinner than he already was.

The driver had his own thing going—a skin-tight silk T-shirt, Jordache jeans, and a pair of black leather fence climbers. Different uniforms of the same tribe. Every tribe had their own look. Silk shirts for the polys, polos for the jocks, band T-shirts under a jean jacket for the bangers. I had put on some accepted version of that banger uniform every morning since sixth grade, never questioning why. Then one day last summer, I did. At first the answer seemed obvious: *It's what I wear.* But the more I thought about it, the more I knew that it wasn't what I wore.

It's what I was expected to wear.

I was a banger and that was the banger uniform, period, end of sentence. A lifestyle sentence, playing a role I didn't remember picking. But does anybody? It happens so slowly that you don't realize it's happening, every tiny decision building the walls. This slang term, that band, this brand of jeans, that hangout. To study or not to study, drink or stay sober, to part your hair on the left, the right, the center, or not at all. Your kingdom-phylum-class-order-family-genus-species down until you wake up one day a banger. Or a jock, or a drama nerd, or a brainiac, or a whatever. And once you're identified and classified and labeled, that's it—you're stuck with it.

But what if you've got this feeling that you aren't your label, that there is more to you than your stereotype, that you don't have to be what everybody says you are? And what if you realize that the same step-by-step path that led you down this dead-end could get you out of it, put you on a whole new road? What do you do then?

I don't know about you, but I made a list.

The polys pushed open the glass doors of the Stop-N-Go, and as they strode past, I was hit by the reek of Jovan Musk for Men, then, smoldering underneath, the faint aroma of pot. They ignored me and I returned the favor, but I kept an eye on the mirror, hoping for a reason to call the cops.

All right, a reason to *pretend* to call the cops.

But no, they just grabbed a couple bottle six-packs of Coors from the cooler. When they put them on the counter, Frank said, "And a pack of Kools. *Box.*"

Just to be a jerk, I said, "Got ID?"

Frank gave a pissed-off sigh that said he was so bored by this punk kid in the white shirt and tie, but he took out his wallet and held out the card for me to see. It was a police ID from California, with Frank's picture and a San Diego address and a birth date that made him nineteen, and other than the picture, it was identical to the one I had in my wallet. He'd obviously seen the same ad sandwiched between the album reviews in the back of *Creem* magazine that I'd seen, sent his $19.95 in just like I had done, getting the same type of plastic-coated, official-looking ID card that I used to buy beer. It was a good fake, and it usually worked in places like the Stop-N-Go where teenage clerks didn't care what you bought. Usually.

"It's fake," I said, struggling not to laugh.

Frank straightened, then leaned in. "It's legit. Just ring it up."

I looked past Frank to the driver. "You got ID?"

"It looks like his," the driver said. Then he shrugged and said, "Come on, give us a break."

What the hell, I thought, *why not,* and was turning to get the cigarettes from the rack when Frank said, "Don't piss us off, asshole—just ring it up."

That sealed it. "Sorry," I said. "I can't sell beer or cigarettes to minors."

Frank rabbit-punched the back of the register, making the bell inside ring. "I ought to bust your face."

I ran a hand under the counter, all easy-like, feeling for the emergency buzzer that would alert George to a problem, but as my fingers bumped against the plastic switch, I remembered that George had taken the batteries out to power the desktop Christmas tree in the office.

Then I remembered the second thing on my list.

I reached down and curled my fingers around the taped end of the broken broomstick we kept under the counter. I heard somebody—me, I guess—say, "Try it," and the next thing you know, there I was, holding the stick out to the side like it was a light saber.

For a second, no one moved. I was sure Frank would swing and it would get ugly fast, ending with me getting beat with my own broken broomstick. Then the driver said, "Let's go. This guy ain't shit."

Frank did a half turn to follow the driver out, then spun back, flinging a six-pack off the counter, three of the bottles shattering, spraying the aisle with glass and beer.

The car was gone before I made it to the door.

It was nine thirty—half an hour yet to go—when she walked in.

It wasn't the way she was dressed. Lots of girls wore designer jeans and boots, and long leather coats were in that winter. And there wasn't anything special about her looks. A Joan Jett haircut and heavy eyeliner. A hundred other girls just like her within ten miles.

But damn, there was something.

Maybe it was the way she carried herself—confident, a little dangerous—or the way she looked into my eyes.

"Can I get a pack of Virginia Slims, please?"

Or maybe it was her voice. A smoker's voice, gargled with whiskey, rough around the edges.

"And some matches, if you got 'em."

I rang it up, watching her as she rummaged through her black leather purse. "Seventy-seven cents," I said. "The matches are free."

She put a buck on the counter. "Nice tie. That come with the job?"

"No. I just like it."

She leaned back, studied my tie-and-shirt combo, and nodded. "Me too."

Pay attention. Here's where it got interesting.

I put the cigarettes and her change on the counter. She pulled out a twenty. "While you got the drawer open, can you break this for me? A ten, a five, and some ones."

I counted out the bills, put them on the counter, and picked up the twenty.

"Thanks," she said. She was putting the bills in her purse when she paused, shaking her head. "I don't know what I was thinking. I already have plenty of ones." She held up a thin stack. "Can I swap these for a ten?"

I gave her a ten from the register and she put it in her purse. I took the ones and flipped through them. "There's only nine here," I said.

She looked up, all surprised. "Oh, sorry." She dropped a one on the counter, then counted out another five ones and a five-dollar bill. "Just give me twenty for all this instead."

I gathered up the bills, putting them all in order and fitting them in their designated compartments in the drawer. When I was done, I held out a twenty. She said thanks and reached for it, but I didn't let go.

"Pretty good," I said.

She looked at me again, something different in her eyes this time.

"If you'd started with a fifty, I would have been suspicious," I said. "But doing it with a ten? That's smart. Most clerks aren't looking to be shortchanged when they see a ten. But if you do that three, four times a night, it adds up fast."

She kept her fingers on the twenty, her eyes on mine. And she smiled. "I believe I'm supposed to say, 'I don't know what you're talking about.'"

Yeah, definitely her voice.

She leaned in and glanced at my nametag. I could smell her cherry lip gloss. "So tell me, Nick. How'd you know? Somebody tip you off to this scam?"

"No," I said. "I did the math."

"Impressive." She smiled at me and gave the bill a tug.

I held on a second longer. Then I let go, too busy watching her to see the line I was crossing. The register would be ten bucks short that night and I'd have to lie my way around it, something I'd never had to do before. Right there that should have told me something.

She took her time putting the twenty in her purse. Then she stood there, hip cocked a bit to the side—*damn*—and ripped the cellophane off the cigarettes, dropping the wrapper in an empty Slim Jim box. "What, no matches?"

I reached under the register and tossed a pack on the counter.

She picked up the matches and put them in her coat

pocket, pulling out a set of car keys. "Have a nice night, Nick."

I watched her walk away. "Thank you for shopping at Stop-N-Go."

She waved over her shoulder as she headed out the door.

I STRETCHED THE phone cord around the corner and into the bathroom, pulling the door shut behind me. Trying not to shout, I said, "I'm at Jay's house."

"What's all that noise?"

"It's the stereo."

"Does it have to be that loud?"

"Mom, it's not that loud. I'm just close to the speaker."

"Are his parents there?"

"They're coming home now," I said. It was true. But they were coming home from Hawaii, and it would be late Sunday night before they arrived.

"What time will you be home?"

"I'm going to crash here tonight," I said. Now, that wasn't true—I didn't know where I'd be sleeping—but Karla told me to plan for an all-nighter, and saying I was at Jay's was as good a lie as any.

"Will there be beer?"

"Not much," I said, and, sadly, that was the truth. Jay's cousins had stopped by and walked out with two cases, Jay declaring it no problem. I saw a problem, but then I hadn't paid for any of it, so I let it go.

"You better not come home with your clothes smelling like marijuana."

The way she said it—*mary-ju-wanna*—made it sound like some exotic, Middle Eastern, mind-altering hallucinogenic instead of the weak homegrown stuff Jay usually had. It didn't matter that I didn't imbibe—everyone else did, and even if you were in the other room, you took the smell home with you. That's why I kept a box of dryer sheets in my room. A couple of those in the hamper and you're all set.

"Will there be any girls?"

Arlene and Vicki were watching TV when I walked in. Frenchy was upstairs making out with Dan-O or Sperbs or whoever it was that month. I could hear Geralyn's insane laugh, and that meant that Cici would be there too. Plus, OP had some girl with him I didn't recognize. So yeah, there were girls there, but not really.

"All right, Mom, I gotta go."

"If you change your mind, you know where the key is."

"I'll be quiet."

"And don't you do anything stupid."

I smiled at that. "I'll do my best."

IT WAS THE part of the night I hated most.

Lights low, windows open for the icy cross-breeze.

Dark Side of the Moon on the stereo. Again.

Empties on the floor, on the steps, on the end tables, the counter. Beer cans, bags of chips, lighters, Zig-Zag packs, McDonald's bags, a pizza box.

Geralyn and Cici on the couch, staring at the album cover like they'd never seen it before, studying every inch in case some secret message that wasn't there last week had suddenly appeared.

Gordie and OP sitting on the floor, talking—like *really* talking, man—about governments and the Bermuda Triangle and this whole Bigfoot conspiracy thing.

Jay at the table, separating the stems and seeds from the weed he bought that day, as focused as he could get on the mindless task.

Karla on the phone, cord stretched down the hall like a twisted orange tightrope.

The Roach, a foot away from the muted TV, giggling, some cop show rerun bouncing colors around the room.

All of them glassy-eyed, slack-jawed, stoned.

All of them but Karla and me.

The first time I got high was in the summer after ninth grade, in the woods out back of Gordie's house. I was a third of a joint in when the panic started, rolling my gut into a knot, kicking my heart into overdrive, seconds stretching into minutes, a moment growing into an impossibly long afternoon of cold sweats and jump-starts, my head crowded with every bad thing that could ever happen, my friends laughing their asses off as I puked, my terror absolutely the most frickin' hilarious thing ever.

It was just your first time, they all said.

Happens to a lot of people.

Well, some.

You'll get used to it.

So a week later, I tried again.

Same results.

It was just your second time.

Happens to a lot of people.

Well, some.

You'll get used to it.

Then it was just my third time, just my fourth, fifth, sixth time.

That was your tenth time, they eventually said. *You better stick to beer.*

I spent a whole year going to parties but not partying, hearing the same jokes but not laughing, watching the same movies but not freaking out, eating the same junk food but not wolfing down the whole bag. At some point, my lack of tolerance became a lack of interest, and then one day I realized that even if I didn't get sick, I didn't want it. And all the fancy bongs and complex pipes and pictures ripped out of the latest issue of *High Times* weren't going to change that.

Because something else had changed.

Me.

And if I could change my peer-driven party-animal self, maybe I could change everything.

As obvious as it sounds, it took me a couple of years to put it all together and come up with my list. The idea, anyway. First in my head—all the things I'd rather be doing than what I always ended up doing; then in the back of a notebook during class—the things that would have to change, starting with the way I dressed, my unofficial uniform, then going deeper, pages of things that I combined or crossed out, distilling it all down to four lines. A new life in eight words. And here I was, ignoring every one of them.

I leaned against the kitchen counter, watching the others sit around, feeling stupid. And boring.

Then Karla came down the hall from the bathroom and hung up the phone, the cord springing back into shape. She looked at Jay sitting at the table, looked into the living room at the others, none of them noticing her, then she looked at me and said, "Let's go."

KARLA WAS NOT a good driver. She didn't drive fast or recklessly, and she never drove drunk. She just wasn't any good at it. She kept one foot on the gas, the other on the brake, took the corners too wide, and didn't always signal. The most unsettling thing—for the passenger, anyway—was how the green '73 Ford Pinto tended to drift to the right when it should have been going straight. The car was four years old and it had 90,000-plus miles on it, but those who had ridden with Karla knew that this wasn't why it drifted.

She bought the car in August, and right away she had me install an eight-track player so she'd have something to listen to besides the god-awful AM radio. It hung below the dash, and when she hit a deep pothole, which she did a lot, the tape would pop to another track, landing in the middle of a random song. The floor behind the driver's seat was littered with eight-tracks, but at night it was always *Frampton Comes Alive!*

Karla had her window cracked open just enough to wiggle her cigarette through. Every time she went to flick the ash, the car jerked to the left, hugging the centerline until drifting back curb-ways. Passengers learned early on to light her cigarettes for her.

I rode with my elbow braced against the passenger door and my right hand wrapped around the shoulder strap next to my head. I could've pulled the belt down and clicked it on like it was supposed to be worn, but if I did that, she'd give me a don't-trust-my-driving? look. Better to just hold on and try not to flinch. There was a pothole thump, and "Wind of Change" jumped back to "Show Me the Way."

She said, "I can't take it anymore."

"Then put the radio on. Or get a cassette player. Those don't skip as much."

"Not that, *this*." She took her hands off the wheel and stretched out her arms, the car inching closer to oncoming traffic. "This town, these people, the same old shit every week. I'm done with it. All of it."

I shrugged. "It's not all that bad."

"Oh, yes it is. You know it too. That's why you've got your little list."

"That's not why I—"

"The only difference is I don't need a list to tell me what to do."

"But the list—"

"We're doing something different tonight," she said, ending the discussion. "We're going to a party up by the campus."

"You invited?"

"No one's invited. You just show up. There's a guy there I want to talk to."

"What am I gonna do, sit in the car?"

"Don't be stupid," she said. "I'm not walking in alone."

"Why didn't you bring Geralyn and Cici with you instead?"

"Three high school girls walk into a college party? It'd look slutty."

"Won't the guy think you're with me?"

She laughed. I didn't think it was all that funny.

"We should stop and get a six-pack or something. It's rude to show up empty-handed."

"We're not," she said, tapping the coat pocket where she carried her stash. "Jay's gonna be about a half ounce off."

THE HOUSE WAS a multi-apartment rental in that part of the city where every house was a multi-apartment rental, and all of them big, with narrow driveways barely wide enough for a car, and wraparound porches that had been closed in long ago to create another rentable room. There were massive trees along the sidewalk, and if there were bushes in the yard, they were overgrown, blocking the first-floor windows. But most of the yards were bare, leaving more room for parking cars and dumping old sofas.

Karla squeezed her Pinto between a tireless Chevy and a new GTO. We followed the reggae beat to the propped-open side door.

"I doubt I'm gonna know anybody here."

"I doubt it too," Karla said, and led the way up the stairs and through another open door, into a crowded space that might have once been a living room. An empty fireplace on one end, a dark wood staircase on the other, and in the middle, two half barrels sitting in an inflatable kiddie pool filled with ice. Above it all, a low-hanging cloud of smoke that smelled of tobacco, sweat, pot, and incense.

Then there was the crowd. A couple years out of high school, tops, but a world away. It started with the clothes. I couldn't tell the jocks from the headbangers, the disco-suckers from the stoners. There were differences, sure: guys with long hair, others with twenty-dollar salon cuts, guys wearing T-shirts, polos, sweaters, even a few sport coats, one guy in a bed-sheet toga, everybody wearing whatever they wanted. I glanced down at my white shirt and skinny black tie. The list was right again.

But more than the guys and their clothes, there were the girls. A lot of them. As many girls as guys, and definitely more than at any high school party I'd ever been to. A few had that big hair thing going, all Farrah Fawcett flips and waves, but most wore their hair parted in the middle if it was long, or brushed to the side if it was a shag. And even though it was forty degrees outside, there were enough girls in tube tops and shorts to make me think of summer.

Despite their differences—or maybe because of them—everybody was talking to everybody else, listening to the same music, hanging around the keg, no group staring down another group, nobody acting all hard, everybody laughing.

It was weird.

Now, I knew that high school had nothing to do with reality, what with all the cliques and sub-cliques and splinter groups, and all the unwritten rules about who was cool and who wasn't worth talking to. And I knew it was all bullshit. But it was the only bullshit I knew. So this was . . . weird.

"I'm gonna look upstairs," Karla said. "You okay hanging out here?"

"I'm a big boy. I'll be fine."

She turned and made her way to the stairs; I grabbed an empty cup from the stack on the fireplace mantel and got in line at the keg. A big guy with a mustache was pouring.

"What are ya drinking?"

I nodded at the keg. "Beer, I guess."

The guy laughed. "Black Label or Odenbach?"

"I've been drinking BL," I said, thinking of the two warm beers I managed to get at Jay's.

"Always stick with who you came with. Ain't that right, Connie?" The guy passed a beer over my shoulder to a hot blonde in tiny gym shorts, then he took my cup, started filling, and said, "So you're a friend of Karla's."

He knows her name? I tried not to look surprised. "Yeah. We, uh, go to the same school."

"She's in *high* school? Damn."

I smiled, no idea what to say to that.

"I'm Eckles," the big guy said, handing me the beer.

"Nick," I said, saluting with the cup. "Cool place."

"Yeah," Eckles said, looking around. "I wonder whose it is."

Another big guy with a mustache staggered into me. "Ecks, you gotta see this."

Eckles motioned to the tap and headed into the crowd, so I started pouring—for a girl who filled a pitcher, another who topped off a fancy mug, a black guy in an ankle-length raincoat covered in band patches, twins in matching hot pants, then a refill for Eckles, a refill for me, "Stop pumping the damn thing, it's all foam as it is," a song I had never heard before was playing, the band shouting that Sheena is a punk rocker, then Andy—*An-deeee!*—passing around a bottle of rum, another pitcher, a keg switch, a pack of foreign-exchange students, then one of the twins coming back, grabbing my arm like we were dancing, then what the hell, dancing to some disco song—disco, for chrissake—then a blues tune, then reggae, back to disco, the girl gone now but me still dancing, lots of people dancing, lots of people spilling their beer and not just me, then back by the keg with Andy and the other twin and the girl who was crying, and then the music got louder and there was more dancing and a crash like something broke and laughing and another keg and that Sheena song again and making out with an ashtray-mouth girl and then shots with what's-his-name and that's all I remembered.

SATURDAY, DECEMBER 17

IT WAS MY BEDROOM.

That much I was sure of.

How I got there?

Not a clue.

And it was my window that was open, letting the cold air in, a shaft of midday sunlight punching me in the eye. I probably deserved it.

And it was my clothes I was still wearing, but that wasn't my jacket on the floor and I didn't recognize the beer mug on the chair. And what was up with all the McDonald's bags?

And it was most definitely my head that was ready to explode. I would have been fine with that if it meant the pounding would stop and the queasy, about-to-puke feeling would go away.

Never again.

That's what I had said the last time too, back in July.

Five months. Not bad.

I should have put *that* on the list.

Speaking of which . . .

STAND OUT.
STAND UP.
STAND BY.
STAND FAST.

Ta-da.

I know, you were expecting more. Something deeper, or at least something that didn't sound like it came from a poster in a guidance office. But you try summing up the person you know you could be in eight words and see if it doesn't end up sounding just as lame. And, yes, I realize it didn't have to be eight words, but I started with the first one, and that sorta set a pattern. After four lines, I'd said everything I needed to say. Besides, as lame as my list was, it was better than what I had before it, which was nothing at all.

Now, why a list? Maybe it was something that had been bouncing around in my head since my freshman history class. Mr. Klock was obsessed with George Washington, and on top of a lot of other things I've thankfully forgotten, Klock told us *all about* this list that young Georgie wrote up describing the way he should live his life. That list was like a hundred items long, and it covered everything from respecting your elders to how you shouldn't kill fleas in front of guests. My list wasn't as detailed, but we were both doing the same thing—reinventing ourselves so we could end up better than how we started. And if it worked for George . . .

The *stand out* part came first, and it wasn't as easy as it sounds. You can officially stand out in high school, but only for unimportant stuff like sports or grades. I wanted to stand out for doing something harder, like not following the herd.

I wanted to *stand up* for the things I believed in. I wasn't really sure what any of those things were, but I assumed I'd figure them out as I went along.

I wanted to *stand by* the people who stood by me. If I ever met any.

And I was going to *stand fast*, stop caving in when it got hard or when it wasn't popular. For a natural-born quitter like me—Boy Scouts, Little League, guitar lessons, karate—that was probably going to be the hardest one on the list, which probably meant it was the one that mattered most.

So that was my list, and I was sticking to it.

Now, where was I?

Ah, yes, holding on to my bed as it spun around the room.

It was Saturday, so my father would be at work and Mom would be out shopping with my older sister, Eileen, and her two kids. They were all wonderfully predictable like that. My younger sister, Gail, could be anywhere, even where she was supposed to be, at Aunt Norma and Uncle Bud's place in Vermont, where she'd been living since last spring. She *could* be there, but I doubted it. Gail was my favorite person in the world with the same last name as me, the only one who really mattered, but I couldn't have dealt with her — or any of them — that morning. Or afternoon.

I took a long shower, first hot, then icy cold until I couldn't stand it. Tony had said it was a proven cure for a hangover, but all it proved was that Tony didn't know what he was talking about. I got dressed and tried to eat something while I ran last night's clothes through the washing machine, including the unfamiliar jacket. The pot smell on the clothes wasn't bad, but there were flecks of dried puke — mine? — below the knees of the jeans. I had to hose off my work boots and set them by the furnace in the basement to dry out.

Definitely never again.

Around three, I left a note on the table: *Went to work.* My shift didn't start for another two hours, but I didn't want to be there when somebody got home. They'd ask questions and I'd have to lie, then they'd find something for me to do, and I'd do it, but they'd end up telling me I did it wrong or that I was taking too long. Better for everybody concerned if I was gone when they returned.

It was warm for December, and the fresh air felt good, even if it did make me cough. I didn't smoke, but I had a smoker's hack. With everybody smoking around me, it was like I had a pack-a-day habit.

I took my time walking. I was in no rush. That and every muscle in my body ached. At least the Tylenol was working on my head. Not so much for my stomach.

Seriously, never again.

GORDIE AND OP were at the arcade, fighting it out on Boot Hill, so focused on moving their boxy pixilated cowboys up and down the screen that it took two rounds for them to notice I was standing behind them.

"Where'd you disappear to last night?"

"Karla and I went for a ride," I said, not sure how much I should share.

OP made with a stupid grin. "You were riding Karla? About freakin' time you got a piece of that."

"Hilarious," I said, not smiling, not in the mood. "We just drove around, that's all."

Gordie dug a quarter out of his jeans and dropped it in the slot. "That's not what Karla said."

OP put his quarter in. "She told us all about the party up by the college. I guess free beer and weed with us isn't good enough for some people."

"When'd she tell you this?"

"Last night, when she came looking for you after you disappeared."

Looking for *me?* Then how'd I get home? This wasn't good. I rubbed the back of my neck and tried to remember. Nothing.

"First you don't give us a discount on the beer," Gordie said, talking louder to be heard over the opening chords of "Let There Be Rock" blaring from the speakers at the back of the arcade. "Then you don't bring anything with you when you waltz in. No beer, no snacks, no pizza, no weed. Oh, I forgot, you're a wuss."

I ignored him and turned to OP. "What time did she come by?"

OP shrugged. "Maybe two? Two thirty? She was all crying, freaked out."

"What'd she say?"

"She said you get stupid when you get drunk. But we already knew that."

My head throbbed in agreement. "Anything else?"

"That you went missing. Like we were supposed to care."

I tried to piece the night together, where I disappeared to and who I was with. Nothing new coming to mind.

OP gave my arm a punch. "*I said,* were there any girls at that party?"

"Just hot ones. Look, if you see Karla here, tell her to swing by the Stop-N-Go. I'm working tonight."

Gordie hit the start button on the game, the four-note theme cycling through. "Karla at an arcade? Never happening." He slapped the joystick and fired off a quick shot, dropping OP's cowboy before it had moved.

"I wasn't ready," OP said as the ghost of Player Two floated up to Boot Hill.

"Yes, you were," Gordie said.

"No, I wasn't."

"Yes, you were."

And that's when I walked away.

I HEADED TO the record store. I scanned the new releases section, then, more out of habit than interest, I flipped through the same stacks of albums I always checked — Queen, the Who, Foreigner, Styx, ELO, Rush. Nothing new. And even if there was, it would be the same old stuff. I was looking for something else. I skimmed the albums on the "HOT SELLERS!" wall and checked the eight-tracks, then gave up and asked the guy at the counter. He smiled a you-get-it smile and pointed me to the punk section.

I hadn't noticed the punk bin before — why would I? I was a banger, and that meant white-suburban, radio-friendly, lighter-waving, one-ballad-per-album-to-show-their-soft-side, endless-guitar-solo, head-banging rock. That's the way the world worked. But my brave new world called for a different soundtrack.

I found it under *R*.

The cover was a grainy black-and-white photo of the band, with RAMONES printed in blocky neon-pink letters across the top. The back cover was a cartoon drawing of a freaky-looking guy riding a rocket to Russia. I'd seen kids do better drawings on desks during detention. I skimmed down the track names to make sure the song was there, and when I saw it, I remembered ashtray-mouth girl, dancing with the twin, mixing Wild Turkey and beer, "Sheena Is a Punk Rocker" still echoing through my poor pounding head.

Best night ever.

Then I remembered that that was all I remembered.

I had what I was looking for and was ready to head to the checkout counter when some deep, dark part of me went back to the record bin, flipping through the rest of the *R*'s until I found it.

Queens of Noise by the Runaways.

All five members of the all-girl band on the front cover, Joan Jett at the far left, staring straight into the camera, her eyes dragging me in. Just like the mystery chick at the Stop-N-Go.

I looked at the cover, then back at those eyes, and for a second I wanted to slip both albums under my coat and walk out the front door.

But I didn't.

I paid for them—$11.96 plus tax—took the bag, and headed off to work.

"START BY TOSSING out all the trash. Don't forget to dig the rotten stuff out of the vegetable bin. It's stinkin' up the place. Then climb in that dumpster and stamp it down so it'll all fit. Don't make a mess out of it. And while you're outside, shovel the slush away from the entrance. Don't go tracking it all back in here, either. When you're done, clean the employee bathroom. Especially that toilet. It's disgusting. Then mop all the aisles and restock the cooler. Might as well do the freezer too. All that shouldn't take you an hour, so no dicking around. When you're done, see me. I got a list."

"Do it yourself, I quit."

That's what I wanted to say. It's what I wanted to say every time George piled on the work just to be a hardass, but instead I said, "Okay," went out the back door, climbed in the dumpster, and started jumping.

Oh, the exciting life of a Stop-N-Go stock boy.

It wasn't an awful job. Mindless, yes, but not awful. A trained chimp could do most of it, but there were probably rules about having a chimp jump up and down in a dumpster, so they hired me. The mindlessness was the best part, though. It gave me a lot of time to think, and over the ten months I'd been there, I'd spent hundreds of hours thinking about four things—sex, girls, music, and moving out, in that order. The first two ate up most of the time, with endless loops of wild adventures starring girls from school, girls who came in the store, or the women in the magazines George hid behind the file cabinet. It was harder to think about music with the in-store radio glued to the Top 40 station. After an hour of Elton John, Barry Manilow, ABBA, and Captain and Tennille, I was ready to chew through a power cord to put myself out of misery.

When Sandra was the manager, it was different. She was older — thirty, forty, fifty, who can tell? — and she was as close to cool as somebody that age was going to get. She smoked in the store, swore more than I did, ordered pizza and paid for it from the register, and you would've had to be twelve for her to proof you for beer, and even then she would've let it slide. Plus, she cranked the radio. It was southern rock, stuff like Molly Hatchet, the Outlaws, 38 Special, and the Marshall Tucker Band, so it was tolerable. She was fired back in August. The cops were involved, and there were rumors that she sold weed at the store, which I never saw but didn't doubt. That's when George got shifted to nights, and the music went to hell.

Moving out had been in my head since my older sister, Eileen, had done it back when I was in sixth grade and she was seventeen and pregnant. She didn't go far, moving in with Aunt Patty, moving home again before Connie was born, then moving out to live with Allen.

Gail got shipped off back in spring, my parents giving up on trying to straighten her out, hoping that living with Aunt Norma and Uncle Bud in rural Vermont would calm her down and put some sense in her head. Or they just hoped it was so far off she wouldn't find her way back home.

The way I saw it, Gail's only problem was that she didn't play by the rules. She had her own, I guess, or she made them up as she went. She was funny as hell and could be really sweet, but, man, could she argue — about anything with anyone — and not just shouting, although she was good at that, too. She'd use facts and logic, and she was a master at throwing your own words back in your face. My parents said she was defiant and belligerent — which Gail saw as compliments — and when she took a swing at a mall cop, they decided that the country air would be good for her nerves. Or theirs. I didn't think Gail was all that bad, but we liked each other, so she took it easy on me. I wasn't there the day they drove her away, but she left a two-word note, written in permanent marker on the wall of my room.

SAVE YOURSELF.

It'd taken me the better part of a year to get started, but I was trying.

My parents thought about me moving out probably as much as I did. They couldn't say hello without asking about "my plans" once high school was over, code for "When are you getting out of here?" College wasn't an option. Not a realistic one, anyway. By the time I realized what I had done—or, more accurately, what I *hadn't* done—I'd picked up enough D's and F's that I'd need two years of straight A's to make it to the low-middle of the grading curve. My father liked to point out—sometimes daily—that a few years in the military might be just what I needed. Joining would be easy. Recruiters were calling twice a week. But the army didn't sound all that different from living at home, only with a lot more rules and a lot less freedom.

When the whole Zod thing went down, you'd think my parents would have been so concerned for their only son's safety that they would have moved to another town. But even at the time, they didn't think it was such a big deal. Easy for them to say—they weren't the ones Zod would be looking for when he got out. Maybe Karla was right. It *was* years ago. If Zod was still pissed, he would have done something by now. He had that reputation. But then he also had a reputation for patience, and I could totally see him waiting a couple years so he wouldn't get the blame if I suddenly had an accident.

But it wasn't worrying about Zod that kept me up at night. What really scared the shit out of me was that I might end up doing nothing with my life. Ever. One thing would lead to another, and the next thing you know I'm getting a dumpy apartment with Jay and Gordie and OP, maybe even Vicki or Frenchy—a bunch of us sharing the space and splitting the rent until we reached a point where we were sick of seeing each other.

Only thing was, I'd already passed that point.

So what *did* I want? I didn't know. I just knew I could do better than this.

Maybe it wasn't about moving out.

It was about moving on.

I WAS KNEELING on the floor, restocking the pet supplies, when I spotted my father in line at the register. I leaned around the display and said, "Hey, Dad," loud enough to be heard over George's fake-friendly banter. My father gave a startled jump, scanning the store for the voice. He spotted me, but I could tell that it didn't click right away. He stepped out of line and walked over to my aisle.

"You're early," I said. "I'm here till closing."

There was an awkward pause and a telling head tilt. Then he said, "Oh."

I could guess the rest.

"I didn't know you were working tonight."

"You're the one who left that note on the fridge," I said, leaving out the details, how he had written that he was sick of me dragging my ass in late Sunday morning, and how he'd be there himself to pick me up, so don't get any smart ideas, mister.

He made an oh-shit face. I kept stacking cans of Friskies cat food, thinking how to play it.

He took a second, then said, "They asked some of us to come back tonight, get some repairs done to the line." *They* were the bosses at Delco. As for *repairs* and *the line,* that could have meant anything. My father had worked there since before I was born, but I only had a vague idea of what he did. Whatever it was, the bosses were incompetent, the new guys were lazy, and the whole place was going down the toilet. At least that's how he described it.

"Technically, we're off the clock, but we're getting comped for it, you know, time off later, leave early on a few Fridays. Hard to pass that up. But I don't want to leave you stranded." That's what he said. The *way* he said it said something different. The Stop-N-Go was a solid four miles from home, and there were no streetlights until you got close to the mall, no sidewalks until you turned onto our street. It was December, and even if it wasn't snowing, it was cold and the wind was howling off the lake. I had a hoodie and that post-frat-party black jean jacket, a pair of cheap gloves, and a black knit cap. And no ride home. But I knew that if I bitched about it now, I'd pay for it later. My parents were already *this close* to charging me rent as it was. Better to act like it didn't matter at all, so I said, "It's okay. Jay was gonna drop by. I'll catch a ride with him."

"Well, as long as you got a ride—"

"Yeah, no problem," I said, the long, cold walk still four hours off. Anything could happen before then. Even Jay dropping by.

My father checked his watch, mentioned again that he'd be at the factory, maybe even all night, got back in line, bought a carton of Tareytons at the counter—which made no sense, since he smoked Marlboros—waved in my direction, and headed out the door. I went back to stacking cat food cans. I was right by the front windows and expected to hear a quick horn toot as my father drove off.

But I didn't.

And that's what made me look out in time to see my father—*waaay* over at the dark corner of the almost-empty parking lot—climbing into our full-size, luggage-rack-on-the-top, wood-on-the-side, impossible-to-miss 1975 Chevy Caprice Estate station wagon, the dome light popping on just long enough, just bright enough, for me to see the woman in the passenger seat.

Then the door closed, the light went out, and my father drove away.

THE WORST PART of the job—other than George—was restocking the freezer.

It was colder outside than it was in the freezer, but I

swear there was something about the ten-by-twelve-foot steel-and-glass box that made it worse. Maybe it was the way the fans blew frigid air right down the back of your neck, or the way the cans of orange juice concentrate stuck to your gloves, or how in the summer you could look out through the frost-coated glass doors and see customers in shorts and tube tops. In the winter you saw people with thicker coats and warmer feet. Or maybe the whole store was built over an ancient Indian burial ground, and this was the portal to an icy underworld.

I fumbled open a box cutter and ran the blade down the top of a case of Green Giant Peas in Convenient Family-Size bags. There's an art to using a box cutter — slice too deep and you cut into the package itself. It was an art I had never mastered. I put the cut-open bag of peas on the shelf marked "Damaged Goods" and crammed the other bags in the case onto the display shelf. After kicking the loose peas into a corner, I moved on to the open space where the yet-undamaged case of TV dinners would go. I rubbed the ice off a spot on the glass and looked out into the store. Down the main aisle I could see the register where George was busy making change for a black-haired, dark-eyed girl in knee-high boots and a leather trench coat.

Her.

I bumped over the stack of boxes I'd set by the door,

yanked open the handle, and stumbled out of the freezer, flinging off the gloves and struggling with the zipper on the Stop-N-Go parka, my fingers too cold to get a grip.

By the time I got the coat off and made it out of the back room, she was gone.

And there was George, recounting a thin stack of money I knew would be ten dollars short, trying to figure out what the hell just happened.

I waited until I was back in the freezer to laugh.

At 11:40 p.m. Geralyn walked into the store. George was taking his second hourlong bathroom break of the night, so I was at the register. I looked at her, then glanced up at the clock over the door. "I thought you couldn't drive after nine."

"Obviously I *can,*" Geralyn said. "Just not legally is all. Where's your boss?"

"Where he always is." I made a loose fist and gave it a shake.

"Uh, disgusting. Give me a pack of Newports."

I reached for the cigs without turning and tossed a pack on the counter, punching in seventy-seven cents on the register keys. I watched while she scraped the bottom of her purse for change, slapping the coins—one by one—on the counter.

"Where's Cici?"

"I don't go *everywhere* with her, you know," she said, then, two dimes and a penny later, "She's in the car. With the Roach."

"No way."

"I wish I was kidding."

I laughed. Cici's standards had hit a new low. "So where you off to?"

"Jay's. Where else."

"Just you guys?"

She found a quarter and that put her over a buck, so she took back some change. "Everybody," she said. "Jay, Tony, Gordie, OP, Dan-O and Frenchy, Sperbs. Louie, maybe. Cici and numbnuts out there. Arlene. Oh, and Vicki."

I nodded as I dropped the coins in the register, hip-checking the drawer closed. That was just about everybody. "I might swing by on my way home."

"Don't bother."

That got my attention.

"We all talked about it," she said. "We don't want you hanging around anymore."

I paused. "Oh, really?"

"Yeah. Really."

"And why's that?"

She shrugged.

I waited for her to smile, make some joke, but all she did was wedge the cigarettes into her purse as she held my stare.

"You wouldn't want to hang out with us," she said. "We're just gonna get high and listen to records. You'll have a lot more fun hanging out with *Karla* and her college friends. They're so much cooler than we are."

So they knew.

I could deny it, laugh it off, but she wasn't laughing, and, besides, the way she said it—putting it out there just like that, smartass sarcastic—well, it sounded about right to me. I looked at Geralyn. I'd known her since ninth grade and we'd had plenty of fights over the years and they'd always blown over. I knew if I said nothing, this too would pass. Same with the other bangers. In a week the whole thing would be forgotten, and, if I wanted, I'd be back, as if I was never gone.

Only thing was, I wanted more.

On my list it said *stand fast,* my way of saying that from now on, I would stop giving up on things just because they got hard, that I'd see things through to the end and not back out. I'd stood fast before, years ago when I agreed to testify against Zod. My parents had told me I didn't have to, but something in my gut told me I did. I remembered how it felt going through with it, and I wanted that feeling again. Giving up now would be easy, but giving up was what everybody I knew did. And look where that got them.

"Anyway, don't bother coming over." She kept her eyes in her purse, shuffling things around, waiting for me to say something. She gave it another moment, then got the hint, slung her purse over her shoulder, and walked out.

I watched her taillights disappear into the night, then looked around the empty store. It felt good to be alone.

TEN MINUTES AFTER midnight, George flicked off the lights, punched 4-3-2-1 into the alarm keypad, and locked the front doors. It was a clear night, cold, nothing but stars and a half-moon. My hoodie and jean jacket were better than nothing, but not by much.

George's rusted-out Gremlin was the only car in the lot.

I knew where George lived. Not the exact address, but the neighborhood. George would have to drive right past the street that led to the subdivision where I lived. A five-minute walk home from there, tops. And I knew that if I asked, George would give me a ride. He wouldn't be happy about it, but he'd do it. But I also knew that George would use the time to run down all the things I had screwed up that night and all the things I didn't get done. Or he'd talk about my lack of ambition or my lousy attitude, how I wasn't gung-ho enough cleaning the toilet. Or, worse, George would get all buddy-buddy, asking me all about school or my family or the girls who stopped by at the store.

An hour walk home or a six-minute ride with George?

I said, "Later," stuffed my hands in my jean pockets, and started walking.

I was in front of the dark liquor store next to the Stop-N-Go when a car pulled into the parking lot, catching me in its headlights. Instead of driving past, the car stopped and the driver hit the high beams. I brought a hand up to shield my eyes. Then a voice I hadn't heard in years said, "Get in."

I thought about running—and I probably should have—but I knew I wouldn't get far. Even if I did, he would catch up with me eventually.

"Let's go," the voice said.

I stood there, blinking, trying to come up with an option.

"Dude, get in the frickin' car."

I willed my legs to move and made my way to the passenger door of the devil-red Camaro. I expected others in the back seat, but it was just the driver. I didn't know if that made it better or worse. I climbed in, the door shutting with a heavy thud.

"Bet you thought I forgot," he said.

His first name was Steve, but nobody I knew called him that. Since middle school he'd gone by his last name, but he was the only one to use the full thing, everyone else cutting Zodarecky down to Zod.

"Admit it," Zod said. "You thought I forgot."

I didn't know the right answer, so I sat there.

Zod smiled. "You were pretty hammered, though. Hell, we all were, weren't we?"

A dim refrigerator-bulb light went on in my head. "You were at that party? The one in the city?"

"Holy shit," Zod said, looking at me, laughing now. "You don't remember, do you? That's frickin' *awesome.*"

I thought back as hard as I could, but my memory bank hit the same blank space as before.

Zod stomped the clutch and shifted into reverse. "You were drunk-tank ready when I got there, but I thought you had sobered up a bit. Kinda chatty for most of it, especially with the ladies. Talkin' tough, too. Well, up until you blacked out."

"Wait," I said, tying the little threads together. "I *talked* to you at the party?"

Zod slapped the steering wheel with both hands, eyes crinkled shut as he laughed. "Dude, stop. You're killin' me."

"I . . . I guess I don't . . . I don't really remember."

Zod popped the clutch and the back tires chirped against a dry spot on the asphalt. "Not even the ride home? The drive-thru? Cutting across that guy's lawn?"

I felt my head shake no.

"How do you think you got in your bed?"

What?

"No way," I said, not ready to picture Zod in my house. Because that would mean Zod knew where the key was hidden and how to find my room. In the dark.

He pulled out onto the main road and punched it, blowing past the speed limit while still in first. "You should have skipped the tequila shots. Those'll get you every time. That's probably why you don't remember telling me how you needed a ride tonight."

"I didn't. My father was supposed to pick me up. But he had to work," I said, a second later adding, "or something."

"Then, it's a good thing I stopped by, ain't it?" He downshifted hard at the curve, the car skipping sideways as he made the turn. "Where to?"

Right here is fine, I thought. *Just let me out here. Then drive off and leave me alone.*

"It's only midnight," Zod said. "We gotta do *something.*"

We? I felt my stomach twist.

Zod slowed as he came to an intersection, rolling through the stop sign, then revving back up to cruising speed. "Get a plate at Tahou's? What do ya say?"

Two grilled hots, macaroni salad, and baked beans, all piled on an order of home fries, topped off with onions, mustard, and meaty hot sauce. The Garbage Plate. Midnight snack of champions.

I said something about it being late and me having to get up early, but the stereo was louder now, cranked to be heard over the red-lined engine, AC/DC wailing on about a problem child.

» » »

"WHAT THE HELL," Zod said, turning away from the counter. "The dude won't take a fifty. Can you break it?"

I looked at the cash in my hand. "I got four dollars and some change."

"That'll work," Zod said, snatching the money, slapping it on the counter, and picking up the tray, all in one fluid move. He cut around the people in line and grabbed an open booth by the door.

I eased in across from him, eyeing the mounded plates Zod was unloading, the grease pooling on the table, turning crumbs into tiny, stale islands. Outside the frost-coated window, women in bright leather jackets and shorts paraded past on nine-inch heels.

A midnight Garbage Plate run to Tahou's Restaurant was a tradition when my grandfather was in high school. But back then, this part of Main Street still had stores and offices, an ice cream parlor right across the street. Now the only legitimate businesses were a pawnshop, a tattoo place, and a twenty-four-hour bail bondsman, the other storefronts dark, burnt out, or boarded up. But there was still a lot for sale on the street, and when a car drove by slow or crept to the curb, the women on the sidewalks let the drivers know what it would cost.

"I love this shit," Zod said, shoveling a plastic forkful of mac salad and hot sauce into his mouth, washing it down with a long swig from a can of Coke.

I pulled a stray hair off one of the hot dogs and flicked it to the floor. "It's all right, I guess."

"Not *this*," Zod said, pointing to our plates. "*This*." He waved above his head, the grand gesture taking in the restaurant. "The stoners, the night-shift workers, the slumming east siders, the preppy college girls." He nodded to the window. "The *working* girls. All of this. I love it."

I took a look around.

In a booth to the left, four black guys in matching parkas and matching scowls nursed coffees. To the right, a red-faced woman with a blond afro chain-smoked Camels. At the counter, a fat man whispered to a wispy Asian girl, one stool down from a sweating businessman who stared at the wall. Drunks staggered in line next to stoners, who read and reread and reread and reread the chalkboard menu, forgetting what they wanted when it was their turn to order. Huddled tight together, the sorority sisters changed their order to take-out, somehow avoiding eye contact with the tall guy in the cowboy hat who kept a running commentary of seedy compliments and bedroom suggestions. Above it all, flicking fluorescent tubes, a pair of slow-moving fans that pushed smoke around the ceiling, and, miraculously, a small swarm of houseflies in the dead of winter.

"It's the ambiance," Zod said. "Nothing phony here. This is just about the only place you'll find it anymore. It's a rarity."

As I watched the busboy crush a bug with the bottom of a ketchup bottle, I thought that rarity was a good thing. Then, despite everything, I dug into the Garbage Plate, unable to resist its spicy-greasy goodness. Five minutes later, I was stabbing the last of the baked beans.

Zod pushed his empty plate to the edge of the table. "Good time last night, huh?"

I nodded, still trying to remember.

"You end up nailing that German chick? The one with the accent?"

German chick? I shrugged, no clue.

We sat there long enough to watch the line form and clear twice, then Zod chugged the rest of his Coke, burped, and said, "I was surprised to see you at that party."

Here it comes, I thought.

He'd been waiting for it.

Waiting for years.

Waiting since the detective told me I had nothing to worry about, that nine months was a long time to hold a grudge.

"Look," I said, "I'm sorry about —"

"Forget it," Zod said. "It was a long time ago, in a galaxy far, far away."

"I just wanna tell you—"

"*I said forget it*," Zod said, a little harder this time. I sensed something, and for a moment wondered if that was what forgiveness felt like.

Zod said, "How'd you know about the party?"

"I didn't. I just came along with a, uh, friend."

"Some friend, leaving you there like that."

"Yeah. Uh, thanks for the ride," I said, still not able to picture Karla leaving me behind or Zod coming to my rescue.

"I figured it was for the best. You weren't making any new friends with those frat boys. Another five minutes and one of them would have taken a swing at you. And you wouldn't have gotten up. They grow 'em big at Pi Kappa."

"Well, then, thanks for that, too," I said, and then yawned, last night catching up with me in more ways than one.

"All right, lightweight, I get the message." Zod climbed out of the booth. "I've got some business to take care of, and you'd only be in the way. Besides, you've got a big day tomorrow. I'm sure you don't want to miss any of it."

I sat there a second, thinking, getting nothing, then I scrambled to follow Zod out the door. On the sidewalk, a woman in red hot pants and a long rabbit fur coat shouted something about a two-for-one offer. I caught up to Zod as he rounded the corner to the parking lot.

"What do you mean I got a busy day?"

"Maybe not the *whole* day," Zod said. "Only the afternoon. If you ask me, don't waste your time. It's not like the score's gonna be any different if you're watching it."

I grabbed Zod's arm, letting go the instant he flinched, his stare telling me not to do that again. "Sorry. I'm just trying to get it all straight in my head."

"The football game," Zod said, fishing for the right key, unlocking the driver's-side door of the Camaro. "Kansas City against Oakland. You took the Chiefs."

What?

Zod got in the car and started it up, then reached over to unlock the passenger door. I dropped into the seat, mouth still hanging open like the idiot I was pretty sure I was.

"I don't know how much you follow the AFC West," Zod said, "but I'm figuring you know that the Chiefs suck."

I didn't know that Kansas City and Oakland were in the same division, let alone their standings, but the matter-of-fact way Zod said it made it seem that Kansas City's record was the kind of common knowledge stat any fool would consider before making a bet.

The car started with a roar. Zod maneuvered by the hookers and pulled out onto West Main. "At least they're giving you three points. Now if it was me, I would have held out for the line at kickoff or eight points, whichever was higher, but you seemed to know what you were doing. Sort of."

I tried to match the bet up with a face, a name. "Was it some guy named Eckles?"

"Maybe. I didn't ask."

"Well, who did I make this bet with?"

"Not so much a *who.* More of a *what.* It's you against Pi Kappa."

"The whole frat?"

"Noooo," Zod said, waving his hand. "Just the ones who wanted in."

"How many?"

"Twenty, twenty-five, tops. But really, it's less a case of *how many* as *how much.*"

I looked at Zod. If my eyes got any wider, they'd fall out.

Zod let me wait as he cut through the sparse late-night traffic, racing under a flashing yellow before turning to meet my slack-jawed stare. "Six hundred dollars."

I laughed. "That's stupid. I don't have six hundred bucks."

"I figured that," Zod said. "That's why I fronted you."

I stopped laughing.

"You seemed confident. You even had those frat guys second-guessing themselves. But in the end they went for it."

"How much?"

"I just told you. Six hundred. Not a bad payday, huh?"

"They won't pay."

Zod grunted. "They'll pay. Trust me. You don't let things that big slide."

"But what if they . . . what if the Chiefs . . . what if . . ." I stopped, unable to get the rest out.

"What if they lose? Then I'm out six hundred."

"You'd *pay* them?"

"Of course I'll pay them," Zod said, downshifting, swerving hard to miss a slow-moving van. "And then you'll pay me."

SUNDAY, DECEMBER 18

It was one thirty in the morning when Zod finally dropped me off.

At first, I tried to fall asleep. That wasn't happening, so I tried to think of anything but football and Zod and the bet, but the more I pretended I wasn't thinking about it, the more I did. I dozed off around four but snapped awake a couple hours later when the neighbor kid tossed the Sunday paper on the front porch. So I lay there, waiting for it to get light outside, and thought about how awesome it would be if I won the bet.

Six hundred bucks.

Decent money. Not millions, but a lot more than I had.

At my whopping $2.65-an-hour job, I'd have to work 225 hours to make that much. Something like that. Given the hours I had, it'd take sixteen weeks—all the way into April—to earn it. Six hundred just handed to you? That'd be sweet.

Better yet, my parents would never know about it, so there wouldn't be any extra ammunition on the you-should-be-paying-rent front. I could spend it any way I wanted. I'd have to be careful, not buy anything too expensive. That would lead to questions, and right away they'd think I was selling drugs. They did anyway, no matter how many times I told them I didn't even *do* drugs. Okay, beer. And liquor, when somebody had it. But not *real* drugs.

I was thinking about all that stuff when it hit me.

What if I lost?

What if the Raiders beat the Chiefs?

Lying there in bed, hands behind my head, my stomach curdling, I thought about that. I wasn't worried about the college guys. They didn't know who I was or where I lived or anything about me.

But they obviously knew Zod.

And Zod knew me.

We had met—if that's the right word—the summer before I started high school. Zod would have been going into eleventh grade if he hadn't dropped out the week he turned sixteen.

Didn't matter. Everybody knew about Zod.

Zod was the one you saw about buying a stereo—still in the box—as long as you didn't ask where it came from.

The one a certain type of girl saw if she was looking to do a "modeling job" for fifty bucks.

The one stoners saw for hash or speed or whatever they were looking for.

Zod was the one I saw stick a knife through a guy's arm.

Saw him good enough to pick him out in a lineup.

Good enough to tell the judge what I saw.

Yeah, I knew Zod.

And Zod knew me.

My hair was still wet from the shower when I came down the stairs and went into the kitchen. My mother, cigarette in hand, looked up from her coupon clipping, little bits of cut-up newspaper and glossy magazine pages littering the table. "Well, what do you know, he's alive."

I got a cereal bowl and a box of Wheaties from the cupboard, a spoon from the drawer, a gallon of milk from the fridge, and took my usual seat at the table.

Mom balanced her cigarette on the edge of the ashtray and picked up her coffee. "How was work last night?"

I shrugged and shook the last of the cereal out of the box and into the bowl, a little pile of Wheaties dust sliding on top.

"How'd you get home? You didn't have to walk, did you? And don't tell me you hitchhiked. I'd rather not know when you do that."

"I got a ride," I said.

"Was it Jay?"

"No, someone else." I knew she'd pry, so I made up the details as I poured the milk. "A kid from school. He asked me to help load some band gear into his van after a show. Then he gave me a lift."

"Was that the same boy who dropped you off Friday night?"

"Yeah," I said through a mouthful of cereal.

She flipped a page in the "Lifestyle!" section, then picked up her scissors and clipped a coupon for some kids' clothing store, doing my sister's work for her again. "That boy, he seemed nice."

I stopped chewing. "You saw him?"

"No. I heard you talking." She glanced over and gave me that look. "You get a little loud when you've had a beer or two."

"Sorry," I mumbled. "Uh, what were we talking about?"

"Oh, I don't know. Something about middle school. And football."

I went back to my Wheaties, but the cereal tasted like cardboard now, and all the thoughts that had kept me awake half the night floated into focus. I didn't hear the car door slam, but my mother did.

"That'll be your father," she said, folding the newspaper section closed. "Did he tell you they had a few of them working all night again?"

"He mentioned it," I said, remembering my father's story, the family station wagon. And the woman in the front seat.

My mother said, "There's something wrong with the assembly line."

Sure there was.

"As if he wasn't putting in enough late nights as it is." She took one last drag on her cigarette and stamped it out as the porch door squeaked opened.

I wasn't ready to deal with my father and was getting up from the table when I heard Karla say, "Morning. Hope I'm not intruding."

I wasn't ready for Karla, either.

My mom had been calling Karla her third daughter for as long as I could remember. She wasn't the only girl in the neighborhood, and she was never really friends with either of my sisters — Eileen was a little too old and Gail was a little too weird — but Karla had always felt welcome hanging out at our place. My mother liked having a girl around who didn't shout at her or tell her how much she hated her and how she couldn't wait to be out of this stupid house. Karla did her share of that, but she saved it for *her* mother and *her* house. To my mother, Karla was the kind of girl any mom would want her son hanging around with — polite without being a suck-up, smart but not arrogant, fun but not dangerous, attractive but virginal. It wasn't all accurate, but when she was around my mother, Karla seemed to change, either playing the role my mother had created for her or not playing any role at all.

"I was just going to pour myself some more coffee," Mom said, all smiles, clearing a space next to her at the table. "You wanna cup?"

Karla shook her head as she sat down, took off her mittens, and unzipped her bright blue ski jacket. Then she looked at me. "Hey, sunshine. You're up early."

I glared and made a low growl, and that made her laugh. But I knew that laugh and the attitude that hid behind it.

"If it's all right with you, Mrs. B, I'm gonna steal your son for a couple hours. I've got some Christmas shopping to do, and I need a pack mule."

"Take him," my mother said. "I'd go with you, but Jerry's gonna be home any minute. He worked all night again. There's something wrong with the assembly line. I guess it's easier to fix it at night."

"Geez, he's gonna be exhausted," Karla said. "We'd better get going, Nick."

I glanced at the clock on the stove. "The mall doesn't open for another hour."

"I know," Karla said, smiling at me as she kicked my leg under the table. "But you know how I hate to be late."

KARLA SWERVED AT the last second and hit the pothole straight on, rattling the front end and launching the Queen eight-track out of the player, mid-song. It was at the "we will not let you go" part of "Bohemian Rhapsody," so I was happy to leave it on the floor by my feet.

It was snowing now, just enough to be annoying, and with every pass of the worn-out wiper blades, a new streak appeared on the windshield. I pushed in the dashboard lighter, and when it popped, I lit one of Karla's Newports, then leaned over and placed it between her lips. It was better — meaning safer — than having her try to light it herself. She drew in a long breath, blew it out sideways toward the cracked-open window, and said, "So how long has he been screwing around?"

I knew what she meant, but I said, "What do you mean?"

"Your father. How long has it been going on?"

I didn't want to think about it, ever, but my brain did the math, counting back to when the late nights started. "Four weeks," I said. And I could have added something about the last time this happened or the time before that, but I let it pass.

"I don't know why your mom puts up with it."

"She doesn't know."

"Oh, please. She's not stupid. The way she talked about it? That whole bit with the assembly line? She knows. She just doesn't care." Karla gave me a glance, the car swerving with her. "I don't blame her. No offense, but your dad's a real bastard."

I could've agreed — and I could've told her to mind her own damn business — but instead I ignored it, the polite way to send a message.

A few potholes later, she said, "So, the other night . . ."

"What about it?"

"Not your finest hour."

I smirked at that. "How would you know? You were *busy.*"

"Not as busy as you think."

"Your friend wasn't there?"

"He was there. We spent the night talking."

"How special."

"Almost as special as your night." She tapped her cigarette ash out the window. "Seriously, what were you thinking?"

"It's no biggie."

She laughed, and this time it sounded real. "You get hammered, then drive off without telling me with the guy you sent to jail for years for *stabbing* somebody, and all you can say is that it's no biggie?"

"*I* didn't send him, the judge did. And it was only nine months. The other four years got added on when he was there."

"Which he wouldn't have been if it wasn't for you."

"He's over it."

Karla shook her head. "I don't believe it. He's not the type."

I reached behind the driver's seat and rummaged through the pile of eight-tracks, knowing that she didn't have anything I wanted to hear.

"Look, you're a big boy, you can do whatever you want—"

"Golly, thanks, Mom."

"It's just that you don't know Zod," Karla said. "You have no idea what he's really like, the kind of *business* he's into."

"And you do?"

She sighed and closed her eyes, the car drifting to the right, jerking back to the centerline when she opened them. "No, I don't know what he's into. And I don't care what he does or what happens to him or any of his little friends, okay? But I *do* care about you, asshole. And for some *stupid* reason, I don't want you to get hurt."

I smiled, liking how her words made me feel.

"Zod's like a . . . I don't know . . ." She looked around for inspiration and found it. "He's like that snow blower over there. He's loud and he's dangerous, but if you stay far enough away, you'll be fine. But if you get too close, and somehow you get pulled in? Not pretty."

"I think you're underestimating me," I said.

Karla took one last long pull on her cigarette, then launched it out the window. "And I think you have no clue what you're getting into."

I WAS RIGHT, she didn't want to go shopping. At least not with me.

We stopped at a donut place—I got a glazed, she got a coffee—and I told her what Geralyn had said, how I was banished and how it probably meant her too. I said it was strange; she said it was about time—both of us wondering how it would play out at school on Monday, neither of us all that concerned.

We talked about the party, about the music and the strange people, the beer, magically avoiding any mention of Zod. I told her I bought a Ramones and a Runaways album, she told me she wanted to see *Saturday Night Fever,* and when I laughed at that, she kicked me under the table, somehow hitting the exact same spot as before. We stayed for an hour, then she dropped me off at the mall and headed to her grandparents' for the weekly Manetti family dinner. I didn't need anything at the mall, didn't want to be there, but it was better than sitting around the house, waiting for my father to start complaining about how hard he had worked last night.

Maybe I'd been wrong. Maybe there was no woman in the car. A trick of the light, a weird shadow, that's all. And maybe there *was* a problem with the assembly line. Things like that broke down all the time. And fixing it at night made sense—they wouldn't have the day shift all standing around, doing nothing. It could happen.

But the comp-time thing? Work a few hours for the promise of a lot more off later? That's where he took it too far. It was a union shop, and even though I didn't know exactly what it involved, I'd heard enough over the years to know that no employee ever worked a minute if he wasn't getting paid for it. Besides, it was the week before Christmas. The factory shut down completely for the holidays. If there were any repairs to be done, that's when they'd do them. And that left me where I'd been since I'd watched my father get in the full-size, luggage-rack-on-the-top, wood-on-the-side 1975 Chevy Caprice Estate station wagon with the strange woman in the passenger seat.

This is why I needed a new life.

Part of it anyway.

I could close my eyes and totally imagine how it would all roll out if I didn't have my list and if I stayed doing what I'd been doing. And what I saw was me becoming my father. I had his genes and looked enough like his old high school photos that it was creepy. Imagining I'd inherit the rest of it didn't seem impossible. He didn't exactly have the kind of life a kid should grow up wanting to have. I'm not talking all the cheating-on-your-wife stuff. I'm talking the stuck-in-a-rut life that was boring to watch and probably worse to live. I'm sure it's not the life he thought he would have, either — I mean, who would? Now, could my list protect me from that fate? I didn't know, but I knew I had to try something, and at that moment, a list with eight words and four lines was the only thing I had.

I wandered the mall, thinking all this through, ending up at Sears, where the store manager told me that the punching bag was for display only. I pulled on my knit cap, stepped out into the snow flurries, and headed for home.

» » »

THE SPORTS SECTION of the paper had the stats.

Oakland Raiders: 10 wins, 3 losses.

Kansas City Chiefs: 2 wins, 11 losses.

The Las Vegas odds makers had the Raiders winning the game by two touchdowns. Stupid enough — or drunk enough — to bet on the Chiefs? You better make sure the other guy was spotting you fourteen points.

I'd settled for a lousy field goal. Three points against a fourteen-point spread? I didn't stand a chance.

The game was in California, and that meant a four p.m. kickoff. Even with my slow, cold walk home, that still gave me two hours to think about it. I could hear Zod's voice saying things he hadn't said yet but would be saying soon, things like, "You owe me six hundred bucks" and "Every damn penny." Eyes open, eyes closed — it didn't matter — I could see everything I saw that night three and a half years ago in the park by the school. Zod, the knife, the blood, all of it playing back, only this time Zod was older and bigger, and this time I was the guy bleeding.

I wanted to clear my head, think it through, plan something, figure out where I'd get the money, but my mind was tweaking and there was nothing I could do but sit there and take it. I told myself I wasn't going to watch, that I'd wait till it was over to find out how badly I had lost, but at 4:05 I was on the couch, clicking through all thirty-six buttons on the cable box, looking for the game. I had hoped that my father would still be in bed, but, no, he was there, a beer in one hand, a cigarette in the other, feet up on the La-Z-Boy.

"Take it easy on that thing," he said. "You're gonna break it changing channels like that."

I slowed, but the shows all stayed the same—ancient black-and-white movies, thirty-minute commercials, ice-skating, reruns of *Gilligan's Island, The Odd Couple, Bewitched, Star Trek, The Brady Bunch.*

My father grunted. "Are you looking for something, or are you just here to annoy me?"

Both, I thought, then said, "I'm looking for a football game."

"A *football* game? *You?* Well, what do you know. Try channel eight."

I hit the button on the cable box and a game popped on.

"There you go," he said. "The Patriots and the Colts."

I shook my head. "That's not the one I want."

"Too bad. It's the only game that's on."

"That's it?"

"This late on a Sunday? That's all that's ever on. Two early games, one late game."

I went back to clicking. "What about the other channels?"

"You're not listening," he said. "CBS and NBC had the early games. They're over. ABC's got the late game, the Pats and the Colts. That's how it works."

I kept clicking. "Is there, like, a channel that just shows scores from other games or highlights or something?"

"Yeah, I wish. Now go back to eight and leave it there. What game are you looking for, anyway?"

"Oakland and Kansas City."

He laughed, which for some reason pissed me off. "You *are* kidding, right? That's a meaningless game between two West Coast teams. The Chiefs are even worse than the Bills—*if* that's possible—and the Raiders will probably win the Super Bowl again this year. Even if they start their benchwarmers, they're gonna walk all over the Chiefs. Now, the Pats and Colts, that's the game you'll want to see."

On the screen, the two guys in beige sport coats were telling all the fans at home what a great game they had in store for them from Baltimore, on this, the last day of the regular football season. I dropped the cable box to the carpet and slumped back on the couch.

"Before you get all comfy," he said, "bring me a beer."

I got up and went out into the kitchen, grabbing my coat off the back of the chair as I walked past the fridge. I was reaching for the back door when my father yelled, "And get a beer for yourself, if you want one."

Outside, snow was whipping down the street. The mall

closed at five on Sundays. It'd be a miserable walk, and I'd get there just in time to turn back home.

In the living room, my father was already bitching about the refs in a game I didn't want to see.

But in the fridge there was beer.

No doubt a bag of pretzels or potato chips in the cupboard.

Maybe pizza at halftime.

I opened the fridge and checked, just to be sure, then tossed my coat back on the chair.

"LET'S HEAD OUT *to Oakland, where Johnny and Steve have watched the Raiders hand the Chiefs their twelfth loss of the season.*"

"Thank you, Roger. Well, Johnny, whenever these two teams take the field, you know that it's going to be a battle."

"How right you are, Steve. And today's matchup was no different. The Raiders came into this game with the division wrapped up, while the Chiefs staggered in with just two wins under their belts. Any way you look at it, the game had no meaning whatsoever."

"Try telling that *to the players!"*

"They were certainly fired up today, Steve. From the opening kickoff to the final gun, every player gave one hundred and ten percent, if not more."

"Let me tell you, for these guys on the field, it was all about pride."

"I spoke to Coach Madden before the game, and he told me frankly he didn't care if they won or lost, he just wanted to get out of the game with all of his players healthy. That's why he let his second-stringers carry the weight today."

"They may not be the starters, but they played like it was the most important game of the year."

"That's the Raiders way, Steve. One hundred and ten percent. And even without their star players on the field, they come away with yet another win, heading into the AFC playoffs next week as early favorites."

"But you gotta hand it to those Chiefs. Sure, they made plenty of errors, but they never gave up."

"No, sir."

"And while they didn't win, they showed that they had plenty of heart."

"A proud team who struggled through a tough year."

"How right you are, Johnny. Well, folks, we're going to send you back to Roger in the studio. So long from sunny Oakland, California, where the Raiders squeak out a one-point win over the Chiefs, twenty-one to twenty."

My father was saying something about namby-pamby kickers and how anybody could miss *two* extra points *and* a field goal in the same game he didn't know, but in the dull roar of a four-beer buzz, all I could hear was the sound of six hundred dollars falling into my lap.

CELEBRATION TIME.

I snuck two more beers up to my room, put on my headphones, dropped *Rocket to Russia* on the turntable, and cranked it up.

Usually with a new album, I'd read over the liner notes on the cover while I listened, but that night I kept the lamp off, letting the red light from the power button and the blue-green glow from the tuner fill the room. There were pops and a hiss as the needle slid to the grooves, then a wash of grinding guitars and a guy singing about cretins and beaches and girls and blasting radios. The songs were fast and driving and each one over in less than two minutes. No deep meaning, no violins or synthesizers, just two guitars, a drummer, and singer, and all of four chords between them. It was raw and real, and I could feel it in my chest, my heart pumping to keep up with the frantic beat.

Six tracks and twelve minutes in, somebody shouted "Go!" and "Sheena Is a Punk Rocker" started blaring, and instantly I was back at the party, jumping around like an idiot, making out with ashtray-mouth girl, having a truly epic time.

Side B was a carbon copy of side A, which made the whole album pretty much perfect. There'd be no going back to the church-choir harmonies and five-minute guitar solos I'd been listening to for forever. I'd found the soundtrack for my new life.

When the last song finished, I flicked on the light and switched *Rocket to Russia* for *Queens of Noise.*

I cracked open the last beer and listened to the title track, leaving the lamp on to get a good look at the cover. It didn't fit the music. The songs were straight-up hard rock, but the photo had the band hanging off of brass poles like strippers in black jumpsuits. I'm sure it was done that way to sell albums, but the looks on their faces told you that they thought the whole idea was stupid, too.

There was one face on the cover I couldn't stop looking at.

Dark hair, dark eyes, shaggy haircut.

Joan Jett.

Halfway through the flipside of the album, it was her voice singing "I Love Playing with Fire." But at that moment, and after the beers, I would have sworn I heard her say, "Have a nice night, Nick."

MONDAY, DECEMBER 19

At Long Pond High School there were two types of senior schedules, unofficially referred to Track 1 and Track 2.

A Track 1 schedule had English, physics, calculus, plus advanced classes in biology and art that weren't even requirements for graduation, with no study halls, no late starts, and no getting out before three p.m. It was the schedule for scholarships and out-of-state colleges, SATs and GPAs, the schedule of choice for brainiac jocks and kids who took French.

A Track 2 schedule met the minimum standards to earn a basic diploma.

If the mandatory courses were completed before twelfth grade—and if at least sixteen elective credits had been earned in classes like home economics, woodworking, and intramural sports—the only things on a Track 2 schedule were English, social studies, math, study hall, and gym. It was the schedule for the chronically absent and soon-to-be-dropouts, JDs and DWIs, the schedule of default for stoners and underachievers.

On the Monday of my first day as an outcast, my Track 2 schedule started with English 12 with Mr. Kerner.

If it had been a study hall or gym, I would have stayed in bed, rolling into school *just* in time for lunch, but if there was any hope of graduating in June—and it was still a mathematical possibility—I had to get at least a D in English 12 every quarter. And since Mr. Kerner was notorious for start-of-the-class pop quizzes that counted for way too much of your grade, I had to show up on time. So when the first-period bell rang, that's where I was.

The other students in the class were jocks and polys, with a few stragglers tossed in. Jay was supposed to be in this class, but by the end of the first quarter, when it was obvious that he didn't have enough credits to graduate this year, they let him drop so he could sign up for Woodworking II. Again.

I hadn't seen any of my former associates since Geralyn came by the Stop-N-Go to tell me I was banished from Bangerstan. If I wanted to see any of them, I knew where to look—back stairwell before school, cafeteria for second lunch, the smoking lounge if they were skipping a class. That made them easy to avoid. My white shirt and tie—standing out and standing fast—were a reminder to myself that I was moving on.

The pop quiz in Kerner's class consisted of three short-essay questions on a poem we were supposed to have read for homework, which I had forgotten all about. Back in September, I would have bullshitted something onto the blank page, but I'd learned that it was a waste of time, since Mr. Kerner gave no points for effort. So while the others got busy writing, I sat there, chin in my hand, and let my mind wander.

Six hundred dollars.

Sweet.

But Zod would probably want some of it.

A hundred bucks? Two? More? *All* of it?

It wasn't like it was mine in the first place.

If I had lost, Zod would have had to pay, and then I would have to pay Zod. At least I didn't have that to worry about.

Because Zod would have made me pay.

One way or the other.

And, let's face it, if Zod wanted to keep all the money, there was nothing I could do about it.

I had hoped Zod was gone for good when the courthouse guards led him away after the trial, but, no, he came back, hanging around the same neighborhood, a disturbance in the Force I could feel but couldn't explain. If Zod decided to walk off with all the money and disappear forever, it would be worth every penny.

When Mr. Kerner said, "You have five more minutes to impress me," my mind jumped back to Friday night at the Stop-N-Go, to the first person in a long time I'd impressed, the girl with the dark eyes and tall leather boots, smoky voice and glistening lip gloss.

That wicked smile.

She'd used me to rip off the store, used her looks to distract me while I let her talk me through the quick-change scam I knew was wrong.

I believe I'm supposed to say, "I don't know what you're talking about."

So cool, so confident.

And she thought *I* was impressive?

There *was* something about her, something real, electric.

Something even Karla didn't have.

Something I wanted.

AFTER ENGLISH 12, I had two study halls, back-to-back, a common feature of a Track 2 schedule.

In my first study hall, I had completed my social studies homework — twenty-five fill-in-the-blanks about the Great Depression — leaving me free to spend the second study hall watching the clock. I could've gotten a pass to the library, reread *The Warlord of Bimskala* again, but it was a Monday and the room was quiet, and it was good just sitting there, brain off, not thinking about anything.

Ten minutes in, the girl behind me poked my shoulder with the eraser end of her pencil.

"You're wanted," she said, flicking her chin at the front of the class.

I expected to see Mrs. Moyer doing that curling-finger

summons, but, no, she was at her desk, playing chess with the exchange student from Finland.

The girl poked me again, aiming her pencil where I should look, the square window in the classroom door where Zod stood smiling.

Shit.

There was no use pretending I didn't see him, not with the way Zod was looking at me. And it'd be stupid now to wait for the bell, hoping Zod would wander off. He'd found a way into the school—a school the court had barred him from entering—and he'd found the *one room* in the building where I was sitting. There was the chance that Zod being there that morning, looking in *that* window, was simply a coincidence. The odds were high against it, though. About the same as a two-and-eleven team beating a three-point spread against the reigning Super Bowl champs. I knew I wasn't that lucky.

A lie to Mrs. Moyer and a pass later, I stepped out into the hall.

Zod's smile was gone. "What the hell you doing here?"

I didn't know if he meant the classroom, the hallway, or the school, so I shrugged.

"All right, let's book," Zod said, walking at a brisk pace toward the fire exit at the end of the hall. As we got closer, I could see the crushed Pepsi can that kept the door from latching shut.

"Excuse me. Did you sign in at the main office?"

I didn't recognize the voice echoing down the hall, but I knew it would only be worse if I stopped to look, so I kept walking. Without turning, Zod raised both hands high above his head, flipping off whoever it was before kicking open the crash bar. His red Camaro sat idling in the space reserved for emergency vehicles.

"I went by your house, nobody there," Zod said, leaving me to wonder if he had just knocked or gone in for a look around. "You know Carol, works up in the kitchen? Skinny bitch about thirty? She called last night, looking for some Black Beauties. I don't normally deliver, but we go way back. I figured that since I was here, I'd see if I could spot you."

Last year, when a bunch of us did a thirty-hour round trip to see a KISS concert in Ohio, Jay had brought along a handful of Black Beauties. I had downed three with a warm beer and stayed up the whole trip, too wired to sleep. Working in a school cafeteria kitchen had to suck big-time. I couldn't imagine how amphetamines would make it any better.

"Carol called someone in the main office, found out where you were supposed to be if you weren't skipping. Figured you'd want your slice of the winnings."

And just like that, it was all good with me. Lying to get a pass, skipping school, flipping off some adult in the hall?

Maybe a week's detention, tops. No biggie. I'd done a lot more time for no money. For six hundred bucks, I'd do it standing on my head.

Wait—a *slice?*

"Gotta hand it to you, either you really know football, or you're just crazy. One way or the other, it worked out. Pretty sweet, huh?"

"I guess," I said.

"This guy I know, he picked the money up for me. No problems. He's got a rep with the frats, so they didn't give him any trouble. We'll swing by his place, get the cash, talk some business, maybe get a bite. Have you back at school by ninth period."

"There's only eight periods."

"Only eight?" Zod shook his head and sighed. "Kids today have it so easy."

As soon as the guy opened the door, I knew it wasn't going to be good.

Part of it was the way the guy was dressed—pointy shoes, black polyester pants, white belt, white silk shirt open to the third button, gold chain with a gold chili pepper–shaped Italian horn. Dressed for closing time at the disco, at ten in the morning.

Another part was the smell—an uneven mix of cigarettes, pot, cheap cologne, wet dog, incense, and whiskey. My stomach rolled with the combination.

Yet another part was the neighborhood itself, one of those places where the city bumped up against the suburbs, with big, old houses next to vacant lots, next to no-name stores, next to bigger houses that had been chopped into apartments, next to run-down churches that used to be packed on Sundays that nobody went into anymore. Some families stuck around, holding on to the community they remembered, where everybody knew everybody, and you watched out for each other. But too many of those families had left, and the people who moved in didn't want to be known and didn't want to be watched. People like the man who opened the door.

But the main reason I knew it wasn't going to be good—the part that really mattered—was the way the guy looked at me when he said, "Who's this shithead?"

"Relax, Reg, he's cool," Zod said, cutting around him to get inside.

Reg glared at Zod as he went past. "He better be."

He was older than Zod by a couple years, taller but thinner, with a droopy mustache, a blow-dry haircut, and a pasty complexion. Reg didn't smile, but if he did, his small nicotine-stained teeth would have given him a grin somewhere between a rat and a wolf. He leaned out the door, glancing both ways down the street, then grunted and let me into the house, locking the two deadbolts behind us.

Thrift-store furniture, no paintings on the walls, a coffee table covered in beer bottles, a TV balanced on a pair of overturned milk crates, a three-foot bong by the end of the couch. Pretty much how I'd expected the room to look when the guy opened the door. What I didn't expect was that there'd be others sitting at the table. Two guys — one short and white, the other black, average height, with a tight 'fro — both of them dressed like Reg, all of them somehow looking alike.

And then there was the girl.

No long leather coat this time, no tall boots, just a V-neck sweater and a pair of tight jeans worn low on her hips, red and black striped socks on her feet, a pack of Virginia Slims on the table in front of her.

Same jet-black shag haircut.

Same magnetic eyes.

Same effect below the belt.

"We'll do this in my office," Reg said. "Your little friend can wait out here." With that, the two guys got up and followed Reg and Zod down the hall and into a room.

When she heard the door shut, the girl smiled. "Hello, Nick."

It was a beautiful smile.

I smiled back, glad that she had remembered my name.

"You here to get the ten bucks I stole from you?"

"It wasn't my money," I said.

"Yeah, but I used you to get it. Some guys would be pissed at that."

I shrugged. "I guess I'm not some guys."

She laughed. "So what brings a not-some-guy like you to a place like this?"

"Picking up some money I won."

"How much?"

"Six hundred."

"You just keep impressing me, don't you, Nick?" She pushed out an empty chair with her foot. "Sit with me."

I sat.

"How'd you win the money?"

"It was a bet on a football game," I said. "Raiders-Chiefs. I took the Chiefs and three."

"I have no idea what that means," she said, smiling the whole time, her eyes—clear, bright—looking right into mine. "But I'm still impressed."

"Don't be. It was a stupid bet. I just got really lucky, is all."

"Then, why'd you make it in the first place?"

"Zod told me that—"

"*Zod?*" She motioned down the hall. "You mean little Stevie back there?"

For years, I had sweated every time I'd heard the name Zod. But the way she said it, with that laugh in her voice, it sounded silly, clownish. She looked away and chuckled to herself, shaking her head. Then she turned back to me. "So, what did *Zod* tell you?"

"We were at a party, and I made the bet with a bunch of frat guys."

"You've got six hundred dollars to throw away like that? They must pay pretty good at the Stop-N-Steal."

Now I laughed. "I don't have that kind of money. Zod covered the bet for me. To be honest, though, I don't remember a thing. Zod told me about it the next day."

She tilted her head down, leveling her eyes. "And you *believed* him?"

I didn't say anything as I thought it through.

"If you lost, you would have had to pay him, not the frat guys, right?"

"Yeah, I guess."

"And you don't remember ever making this bet, or who exactly you made it with."

"Nope."

"Sounds like a scam to me," she said. "You lose the bet, he gets paid. You win, he tells you it was just a joke."

"Then why did he bring me here to get the money?"

She tapped a cigarette out of the pack, flicking a BIC to light it. "That's the part I don't get."

"I'm sure he'll keep some of it. Maybe most of it. He's the one who took the risk."

"I think you're wrong about that," she said. "But maybe it'll still work out for you."

"Why wouldn't it?"

She took a long drag on her cigarette, blowing the blue-gray smoke out slow and even, watching me the whole time. "Things don't always work out the way you want."

Then the door opened down the hall, and her smile disappeared. She sat up, crushing the just-lit cigarette in a glass ashtray.

The black guy led the way. Right behind him, Zod was talking over his shoulder, his words rushed together, his voice almost giddy. "You know the Klassy Kat? Over by the airport? I know *all* the girls. Smokin' hot, every one of 'em. There's this one—Chastity—she's a fox and a half. A redhead, too—and you know what they say about redheads."

Reg came down the hall last, brushing a knuckle along the bottom of his mustache. His eyes were pin-prick sharp, and they darted around the small room.

"You should check it out, Reg," Zod was saying. "Tell Chastity that you're a friend of mine. She'll treat you right."

In a cold, flat voice, just above a whisper, Reg said, "I don't touch whores."

"Naw, Chastity's not like that. She just likes to party, that's all. Seriously—"

"And I don't have any friends," Reg said. Then he looked at the still-smoldering cigarette in the ashtray. "What I tell you about smoking in here?"

"I forgot," the girl said, and even though she rolled her eyes as she said it, I still heard the quaver in her voice.

"You forget a lot," Reg said. Then he looked at me, stared me down. "Hey. You. Shithead. You hittin' on my girl?"

I felt my mouth drop open.

"I asked you a question," Reg said. "Are you hitting on her?"

My throat went dry. "No, uh, honest, uh, I, uh, I was—"

Reg stared hard, his eyes narrowing as he leaned forward. Then he laughed. "Check out Mr. Casanova here, looking to get busy in my house."

The others laughed at that. The girl studied her fingernails, her bored expression telling me what she thought of it all. Reg grinned as he put his hands on the girl's shoulders. "What do you think, babe? You going to run off with this kid?"

She waved a finger around the room. "And leave all this?"

Reg's smile flickered. "Don't be sarcastic, Dawn. It makes you sound stupid."

Zod slapped me on the arm. "Come on, *Mr. Casanova.* I gotta get you back to school."

I glanced back as we headed out the door, half expecting

to see Reg glaring at me, but he was still looking down at Dawn, his smile fading, her smile gone.

"— USED TO MOVE a *lot* more stuff than he does now. The higher-highers are getting annoyed. And he's doing way too much product. Makes him paranoid. He thinks everybody's plotting to — *Dude, crank that song* — gotta play Zeppelin LOUD. '*I am a traveler of both time and* —'"

I turned it up and kept my eyes on the road. One of us had to. Zod raced on, talking as fast as he was driving, all over the place, jumping topics and switching lanes, redlining every gear of the cocaine-fueled ride.

"— and the black dude? He used to be Reg's muscle, but he got all into this Rasta non-violence crap. That's how I got the job."

The kids I knew didn't do coke. Not that they didn't *want* to, just that it was so expensive. You could buy a week's worth of weed for a couple hours' worth of coke. They might be failing math, but even they could figure out the economics behind that one.

"So she's like all, call me and we'll get — *Look at this bitch Toyota, cutting me off.* I should ram his precious — Yeah, that's right, I'm flippin' you off, what're you gonna do about it, old man? Yeah, that's right, look away, chief — Whoa, yeah, shit, bro, I almost forgot," Zod said, laughing, slapping the steering wheel with both hands. "You *called* it, bro. Frickin' *nailed* it. *Nobody* took the Chiefs. Brilliant move, dude. You scored, *big-time*." He reached inside of his coat and pulled out a white envelope, tossing it on my lap.

I pick it up, pulled the flap free. Inside was a white piece of paper, folded into a tight, three-inch-square origami packet. I pinched the packet and could feel the crystal grains shift. I knew exactly what it was, but when I put the packet back in the envelope, I said, "What's this?"

"It's three-point-five grams of Peruvian rock. It ain't pure, but it's only been stepped on a couple, three times."

I set the envelope on the armrest between the front seats. "No, thanks."

"Hey, that's not a gift," Zod said. "You earned it."

"I don't want it."

He laughed. "Yes, you do. You just don't know it yet."

"I don't do coke," I said. Then — because *stand fast* was on my list — I added, "I don't do any drugs at all."

"Abstain all you want, Mr. Clean," he said, still laughing. "You can sell the shit. You got three-fifty, four hundred bucks right there."

"I'm not selling drugs."

"Give it away, then. Find yourself a couple east-side girls. Get laid all weekend on that packet. It's your share of the winnings — you can do whatever you want with it."

"I'd rather have the money."

"That *is* money, dickhead. You just gotta make the exchange. With the cokeheads at your school, you could unload that before the last bell."

"I'd rather have—"

"And *I'd* rather you *quit your bitching.*" He slammed his fist down on the dashboard. "I backed your sorry ass when you made that bet, and *this* is the thanks I get? I go halves with you—fifty-frickin'-fifty—and but that ain't good enough. No, you gotta have *everything* perfect. Well, *Nicky,*" he said, teeth clamped tight together, "life ain't like that. You won it, you take it. Do whatever the hell you want with it."

I sat there, looking straight out the window, waiting for a sucker punch to the side of the head. Or a knife through the arm. Enough mumbled words cut through the blaring music to let me know he was considering both. Five semi-silent minutes later, Zod turned onto the access road that led to the back of the school. I reached over and picked the envelope up off the armrest. "This is my share, right?"

"That's what I've been trying to tell you," Zod said in a mocking, singsong voice.

"And I can do whatever I want with it?"

"Yeah, go crazy."

I tapped the envelope against my leg and thought it through.

Two months' worth of pay at Stop-N-Go wages in a packet that weighed less than a couple sticks of gum.

I definitely knew kids who'd buy it. Polys mostly, but a few of the jocks, the muscle-heads who'd snort it between reps at the gym. The stoners stuck to pot, but they might buy it to trade up, score some sensimilla or Thai stick. And there were plenty of people who came into the Stop-N-Go who asked if I had "anything, you know, behind the counter," and others who'd straight-up say they were looking to buy drugs. They'd pay decent money to take the stuff off my hands.

It would take some time, but I could probably get four hundred for it.

Then again, I could sell it for three without breaking a sweat. At that price I could sell it in five minutes just cutting through the smoking lounge at school.

I took a deep breath to settle myself.

Maybe I'd regret it later, look back on it as a stupid mistake, but at that moment, riding in Zod's devil-red Camaro, Led Zeppelin blasting on the radio, I knew it was the smart thing to do.

"Here," I said, holding the envelope out to Zod. "It's yours."

Zod looked at me. "What d'ya mean?"

"I can do anything I want with it. I'm giving it to you."

"Dude, don't be stupid."

"You said it's mine to do with what I want, right? Well, I'm giving it to you."

"What do you want?"

"Nothing. I'm just giving it to you. You backed me at the party, gave me a lift," I said, making it up as I went. "I figure I owe you."

"You're an idiot, dude," Zod said, "but I'd be a bigger idiot not to take advantage of your stupidity." He took the packet and shoved it deep inside his puffy down jacket as the Camaro pulled up to the service entrance of the school. The car rocked to a hard stop and I made to get out, but before I moved, he put his arm out across my chest. "Hold on a sec."

"We can't stay here," I said, scanning the nearby faculty parking lot for any roaming teachers. "If we get caught—"

"Shut up and listen. I need you to do me a favor." He reached in a different coat pocket and pulled out a clear box of Tic Tacs, but instead of little white mints, it was filled halfway with triangle-shaped blue pills. "Give these to Carol up in the kitchen."

"I don't know which one she is."

He dropped the box in my lap, the pills rattling inside. "Skinny white chick, got Carol written on her shirt. You'll find her."

"Students aren't supposed to be in the kitchen area, plus if I get—"

"You're not supposed to skip school to be picking up drugs you won in a bet, either." He revved the engine and waited for me to make my move. I could've done a lot of things, but what I did was open the door and climb out. Resting an arm on the roof, I leaned back in. "Now we're even, right?"

Zod's smile melted into a smirk. He popped the clutch, and the passenger door slammed shut as the Camaro launched back down the access road.

WEDNESDAY, DECEMBER 21

KARLA SET THE PIZZA BOX ON MY LAP. "I BROUGHT YOU A slice."

I'd been waiting more than twenty minutes, and my ass was nearly frozen to the guardrail behind the Pizza Hut. I was so cold, the oven-hot cardboard only felt warm. Inside was a medium pizza with double portions of every topping the place offered. "That's a big slice."

"There's more for your gut . . . at the Huuuuuuut."

It was off-key and the words were wrong, but I recognized the jingle from all the late-night commercials. "Thanks."

"It was a prank order. We were gonna toss it anyway," Karla said, shrugging like it was no big deal. She took out her cigarettes, lit one.

I nodded at the restaurant. "What's it like in there tonight?"

"Slow. Some families with bratty kids, breaking all the crayons. Some blue-hairs from the nursing home. I'll be lucky to make five bucks in tips." She turned her head and blew the smoke behind us, gave a little cough, and said, "I'm moving to Florida next week."

Bam.

I took a breath, felt my chest tighten, then went back to wiggling a slice free, lifting it straight up, the mozzarella stretching with my reach, and the mounded-up toppings sliding off the sides. I swept a finger around the slice, snagging the mozzarella strings, looping them around, keeping my focus on the pizza.

I could feel her stare.

She waited until I had taken that first big bite, until my mouth was full, the cheese clinging to my lips, before saying, "Wow, Florida! How exciting! I'm so happy for you, Karla."

I chewed faster.

"What, you gonna pretend you can't hear me now?" She took an angry drag on the cigarette. "You can be such a baby, you know that?"

I swallowed hard. The scalding lump stuck halfway down for a dozen heartbeats before dropping into the empty pit that was my stomach. I took in a shallow breath. "When's this?"

"We're leaving Christmas morning."

"Who's *we?*"

"*Who do you think?* Me and Scott."

I remembered the first guy Karla dated. Mike something, way back in sixth grade. That lasted almost a month. Then there was that kid from her church, then nobody for a while, then Redhead Randy, then Joel, then the Korean exchange student. The first time she went all the way was with a guy from Hently, in the parking lot behind the Cineplex on their one-and-only date. Since then there'd been a steady string of guys, a few years older, all of them with names I'd heard, since Karla didn't have a girlfriend she could trust and she had to talk to *somebody*. It had been that way for years, our friendship built on her telling me things I'd rather not hear, me letting her talk, letting her cry on my shoulder the rare times it got to her. And now she was moving away. With Scott. A guy she had never mentioned.

I took a smaller bite of the slice. Despite all the toppings, there was no taste to it now. "Why Florida?"

"Scott's brother lives in Venice. Got a place four blocks from the ocean. He's getting Scott a job at the hotel where he works. He thinks he can get me in as a waitress."

"Hmmm."

She blew smoke out across my face. "What the hell's your problem?"

I took another bite, mumbling a *nothing* as I chewed.

"Aren't you happy for me?"

"I am," I lied. "It's just that it's, you know, sudden, is all."

"No, it's not," she said. "Scott and I have been talking about it for a month."

A month? Damn.

"And you know Scott. Once he gets an idea in his head . . ."

No, I didn't know Scott, and I didn't know what was in

Scott's stupid head. But knowing what most guys thought when they looked Karla up and down, I had a pretty good guess.

She closed her eyes and stretched her arms out above her head. "This time next week, I'll be on the beach."

This time next week.

How many times had we sat like this, side by side?

How many weeks?

How many different places?

All the talking we did, all the talking we didn't *have* to do, not having to say anything just to fill the space. All the nights I lay alone in my room, thinking about her — no, fantasizing about her — wishing we weren't "just friends."

I glanced over at her.

That twenty-dollar Farrah Fawcett haircut.

That stupid Pizza Hut hat.

Too much blue eye shadow, too much Windsong perfume.

Her smile dulled by all the Newports.

Still.

More beautiful now than ever before.

And at that moment, the only friend I had.

I felt my jaw tighten.

Fine.

Book out.

Piss off.

Go.

But first . . .

"What are you gonna do when this Scott guy screws you over?"

She opened her eyes and gazed up at the clouds, then closed them again, shaking her head. "That isn't going to happen. Scott's not like that."

"Yeah, right. Isn't that what you said about Garry?"

"He's nothing like Garry—"

"Or Steve? Remember Steve, the one who stole your mother's purse?"

"Let's not—"

"Or that guy Todd? Him and his twin brother? Remember them? Remember that party?" I tossed the half-eaten slice into the box, then flung the whole damn thing over my head, the pizza landing in the snow with a muffled *thump.*

I could tell she was looking at me, and I braced for a shouted one-sided argument, but instead she hit me with a half-whispered question. "Can't you just be happy for me?"

I sighed, stared at my hands. A minute later, "All I'm saying is—"

"I know what you're saying. But I have to do this. I have to get on with my life."

"You don't have to move away to do it."

"Yes, I do. If I stay here, nothing will change and I'll fall in the same rut everybody else does, and that'll be it. No, if

I'm ever going to get my own life, I need a fresh start. And I'm not going to find it here."

I wanted to say something, but I couldn't put the words together, couldn't put a *thought* together.

"You got your list, the things you want to change in your life, right?"

I grunted.

She stood up, brushed the snow off her ass, and started for the back door of the Pizza Hut. "Did you ever think that maybe I had one too?"

WALKING HOME, hands stuffed in my pockets, head down watching for ice patches on the sidewalk, stomach growling, and thinking about Karla and that pizza I tossed, I didn't see the car until it was too late. But there it was, on the wrong side of the road, pulling up to the curb next to me, Zod's devil-red Camaro.

"Get in," he said.

I stayed on the sidewalk. "Thanks, but my house is right up here."

"I *know* where you live. Just get in the damn car."

Running was an option — not a good one, but an option. So was walking away. I glanced down the street to my house, then got in the damn car.

He said, "Any problems getting that stuff to Carol?"

"If there were problems, you think I'd be sitting here?" It

came out more sarcastic than I had meant it to, but he didn't seem to notice.

"You got balls, Nicky. I'll give you that." He revved the engine, then raced down the short street to power-slide around the corner. "I knew it when I heard you make that bet with those frat boys. I said to myself, 'That kid's got balls.'"

Ah yes, the bet. It all came back to that. If it ever happened.

Zod took a drag off his cigarette, blew it out. "No. Before that. Years ago. In court. Remember?"

I remembered.

"I was a real badass back then. Thought I was *sooo* tough." He moved his hand like it held a knife, stabbing the air as he laughed. "Funny thing, dude? *You* were the tough one."

I looked around. *"Me?"*

"Hell yeah, you. Going to court, pointing me out. You *had* to know I'd be looking for you."

And here it comes, I thought, bracing myself, ready to pop the door open and roll out.

Zod laughed again. "I would have, too. But I got locked up. And once I got in there, well, I found a few ways to get in trouble all by myself. By the time I got out, I had a whole new perspective on lots of things. Like you."

I felt for the metal end of the seat belt. A poor weapon, but it'd be something.

"Turning me in like you did," Zod said, "that took balls.

I realized I had to respect that. Then I start hearing things about you, how you wouldn't let your friends take stuff from the store, that you don't get high, but that you're not a dick about it. I had to respect that, too."

Not what I expected. And I didn't expect to like hearing it so much.

"Okay, enough memory-lane shit," he said, saying it in that jokey now-back-to-business voice teachers like to use. He downshifted hard, slowing to the speed limit as he went by the stop sign. "You know Jumbo, right?"

It was a weird question, and it took a second to realize he wasn't talking about the Disney elephant. I shook my head.

"Yeah, you do. The fat guy at Mr. Pretzel. You know who I mean."

I did. At four-hundred-plus pounds, he was hard to miss. He worked at the soft pretzel kiosk near the record store in the mall, and by work I meant he sat on a stool by the counter and watched girls go by. I didn't know that was his name, but it fit, even if the elephant was smaller.

"There's a paper bag on the back seat. I'll drop you off at the entrance by the camera shop. Go to the pretzel place, give Jumbo the bag, he'll give you four hundred. Be sure you count it. Twice. I'll pick you up behind Woolworth's. And get me a large pretzel with cheese."

I laughed. It was that stupid.

"No way. I'm not running drugs for you. I don't care what you say. Forget it."

He sighed, all dramatic. "You're not *running* drugs—you're dropping them off is all."

"No, I'm not."

"Look, it's simple."

"Then you do it."

"Can't. I'm barred from the mall," he said, his voice somewhere between sarcastic and pissed. "And Jumbo needs his weed."

"Well, I'm not doing it."

"Yeah, you will, so stop pretending. I'll give you twenty bucks."

"I don't want your—"

"Aaaannnd . . . I'll call us even."

My list said *stand up,* and saying no to Zod was the kind of thing I should stand up for. But the thought of having Zod out of my life? Too good to pass up.

"For real? That's it, we'll be even?"

"Sure," he said. "I backed you at the party; you're helping me out now. We're cool."

So I did it.

I thought I'd puke the whole time, and when I stood there counting all those bills at the pretzel counter, the cold sweat soaking my shirt, my hands shaking, I was sure the mall cops would bust me. But they didn't, and five minutes later I was in Zod's car, heading toward my house. I didn't laugh when Zod joked about me forgetting his pretzel, but I lost it when he did this impersonation of Jumbo.

I didn't want him thinking that I enjoyed any part of it or that I'd ever do it again.

So why did I say, "Thanks," when he handed me that twenty, and, "See you around," when he dropped me off at home?

SATURDAY, DECEMBER 24

"START WITH HAULING OUT THE TRASH. YOU'LL HAVE TO shovel the snow off the dumpster first. Be neat about it for once. While you're at it, clear all that slush away from the back door. And don't make a frickin' mess this time. When you're done with that, some punk kid pushed a six-pack of Odenbach off the rack in the cooler. Just reached in and shoved it. Punk's lucky I didn't catch him. Anyway, there's beer all over everything in there. And don't go and get cut on the glass. The last thing I need is you bleeding on the produce. When you're done with that, see me. I got more."

GEORGE WAS RIGHT—there was beer all over everything. Odenbach VTO Premium Lager. Top shelf, of course, so when the bottles hit the metal floor inside the cooler, they exploded, spraying the cramped space with glass and beer. There were also a dozen broken eggs, but by the look of them, they'd been there for much of the day.

I shook open a plastic bag and started with the soggy six-pack carton, then moved on to the bigger pieces, taking my time so I didn't slice off a finger on one of the shards. That, and the longer I spent in the cooler, the less time I'd have to spend listening to George and the nonstop easy-listening Christmas music.

Another brainless Saturday night at the Stop-N-Go.

Which capped off another brainless week at school.

It was the week before vacation, and nobody wanted to be there. Not the students, not the teachers, not the maintenance workers—not even Mr. Kerner, who was happy to let us catch up on our sleep while he played Beatles records and graded papers.

The study hall monitors were giving away passes for the asking, and I'd taken every one offered, more out of habit than need. I'd planned to crash in the library, but both Thursday and Friday it was filled with squealing freshmen. I could've hung out in the cafeteria, but the smell in that airless, sweaty room was always nauseating. The smoking lounge was just as bad. Besides, there was nobody in either place I wanted to see.

In the end, I'd wandered the halls for two days, sitting alone in stairwells, rereading the paperback copy of *The Warlord of Bimskala* I'd had since eighth grade.

I'll be honest, I'd bought the book because of the cover—an exotic, olive-skinned woman leaning against a marble pillar, gold bracelets up her arms, a little tiara in her flowing black hair, a chainmail bikini that barely covered her tight body, and a pair of breasts that ignored the laws of gravity. But what sold it was the look of raw get-over-here lust in her dark eyes. It was a look that my thirteen-year-old self didn't really understand but instinctively obeyed.

Oh, and there was a guy in the picture too. Lots of muscles, bloody sword in one hand, laser pistol in the other, the look on his face saying that he didn't give a damn what they threw at him. Jack Morgan, the warlord from the title. Still, not as interesting as the princess.

I had second thoughts about buying it when the store clerk told me it was a "classic," which is librarian-speak for boring, but the princess stared me down, and as soon as I got home, I dove into the book.

It took me an hour to get through the first two chapters.

That pulse-pounding cover was covering up for a painfully slow story filled with impossible-to-pronounce characters, an SAT-level vocabulary, and zero sex. I had stayed with it, though, and by the middle of the book I could follow the plot enough to keep up with the warlord and, more importantly, the half-dressed princess.

Since then, I'd read the book a dozen times, and each time it was easier to swap out Jack Morgan and stick myself in the story. The plot still dragged, but there were some decent battle scenes that I could imagine joining in on, heroically taking on the evil villain's army. As for the missing sex scenes with the princess, I had no problem imagining myself in those, either.

So there I was, sitting in the stairwell, rereading the book I pretty much knew by heart, when it hit me.

This was where my list came from.

The way Jack Morgan acted in the book, the things he did that made me cheer him on? They were the same things that I thought I'd come up with all on my own. The more I thought about it, the more it became obvious.

In the book, the hero stood out, mostly because he was a six-foot-tall Texas Ranger who woke up one day on another planet where people averaged just over five feet — don't ask, it's too crazy to explain — but he was different, and that made him more interesting.

The hero stood up, defending the people of Skalopios by leading an army of flying walonks against the dark forces of Castle Symarip. Yeah, it all sounds stupid, but here's the thing — when it came down to it, when someone *really* needed him, the hero was there.

The hero stood by the princess, which sounds easy, but she was being hunted by assassins, and the princess's evil twin sister was doing everything she could to lure him away. But he stayed by the princess's side, even when she had to flee with nothing but that silver metal bikini.

Jack Morgan stood fast, sticking with the attack he and his flying pals launched, even when it looked like it may get them killed. It didn't, and in the end they won, but he didn't know any of that at the time, just that he had to see it through.

Stand out. Stand up. Stand by. Stand fast.

My big plan for the rest of my life, stolen from the pages of a sixty-year-old fantasy novel.

Did it make my list stupid, or did it prove it was inspired? I didn't know, but I wasn't going to give up on it yet.

JUST BEFORE TEN, George buzzed me to the register and told me to take over, that he had some important calls to make back in the office. That meant that he would spend the next forty minutes in the one-toilet bathroom, just him and his *Hustler* magazines, and that was fine with me. George could sit in there all night. At least he'd be outta my way.

It was snowing like crazy outside. There'd be a white Christmas, whether we wanted it or not. The few customers who came in were stocking up on the basics—milk, bread, diapers, cigarettes, beer—in case the storm dumped more than the predicted five inches. I didn't expect to see anybody I knew that night, and then in walked Karla.

She shook the snow off her knit cap. "People who don't know how to drive should stay off the road."

A week ago, I would have jumped on that, making a joke about her driving or asking if that's why she decided to park, but now I just said, "Yeah, it sucks."

"I can see maybe going a *little* slower, but come on, people, *thirty* miles an hour?"

"The speed limit's thirty-five."

"I know. They're crawling out there." She smiled at me, and I tried to smile back, but it wouldn't stick, the corners of my mouth fighting me to stay pissed.

"Your boss in the back?"

I nodded.

"You busy?"

I shook my head.

"Hey, listen," she said, stepping up to the counter. "I know you're upset at me for leaving—"

"I didn't say that."

"But you are, right?"

I grunted something, then got busy pretending to straighten the candy next to the register.

She sighed. "I don't want it to be like this between us."

"Like what?"

"Like *this*. All . . . all *distant*. Like I'm gone already."

I nudged the Tic Tac display a tad to the right, slid the cheese cracker packets forward.

"We've been friends since fourth grade. That shouldn't stop just because I'm moving to Florida."

I took the cellophane wrapper off the tray of Life Savers, moved it closer to the gum.

"Florida's my chance to start fresh, you know?"

I scraped an old piece of masking tape off the top of the register with my thumb, flicked it toward the garbage can by the door.

"But here, in this town, I mean, I feel like . . . like I'm . . ." She looked around as if the answer was on a shelf. "I'm *trapped.* Nothing's gonna change for me here. Not for me, not for you, not for any of us. We're stuck. And I'm scared that if I don't go now, in ten years I'll still be here, still working at Pizza Hut, still living at home, still—"

"You should buy a hat."

Karla looked at me, tilting her head that cute way she did when she was confused.

"A big one. The floppy kind," I said, still scratching at the register. "The sun's different down there. And you get burnt up here as it is."

She smiled. "Yeah," she said, slower now. "I do, don't I?"

"You'll get all burnt, then you'll start peeling, and when you do, you look like some leper, skin dropping everywhere—"

She laughed and, after a moment, so did I. "Okay, okay," she said. "I'll buy a hat. A *floppy* hat. Geez."

I looked across the register, looked into her eyes. "I'm gonna miss you."

Karla reached out and threw her arms around my neck, pulling me close, leaning over the counter to do it, packets of Life Savers rolling off onto the floor. I felt her face against mine, smelled the perfume she always wore. I closed my eyes and hugged back. I wanted change, and now I was getting it. My best friend leaving town, my other friends probably wishing I would go with her, drug dealers asking me for favors, and me doing them. I hugged tighter, wondering what would happen next.

"It's gonna be okay," Karla whispered. "You'll see. It's gonna be the best year ever."

THE LIGHT BLUE Trans Am pulled up just after ten. Frank Camden climbed out of the passenger seat, said something to the driver, slammed the door, and headed into the Stop-N-Go.

It was last week that Frank had pushed the six-pack of Coors off the counter when I had laughed at his phony ID, but by the way he nodded as he walked past the counter, saying, "Hey, how's it going?" it was clear Frank didn't remember any of it.

I watched him in the round mirror, and as Frank studied the cooler window, I studied him.

Silver and black silk shirt, red polyester bell-bottoms, wide belt with a silver buckle, black platform shoes that made him two inches taller, feathered-back hair with every damn strand in place.

Look up *poly* in the dictionary and there'd be Frank.

He stood with the cooler door open, making up his mind, deciding on two twelve-packs of Löwenbräu. The most expensive beer in the store. Frickin' private school east sider.

I was thinking through how to play it — tell Frank to piss off as soon as he set the beer down or wait until he handed over that fake ID? — when, from down the aisle, Frank half shouted, "That was one bitchin' party, huh?"

Okay, I wasn't expecting that. And it must have showed.

"Last week, Flint Street?" Frank set the beer on the counter. "Babe city."

"Flint . . . ?"

"The college party," Frank said. And smiled. Not a sarcastic asshole smile. A real smile. I still didn't like it.

"You were hanging out with Andy and those twins when I got there. Probably didn't even see me — the place was mobbed."

"Yeah, it was pretty crowded," I said, trying again to remember any of it.

"Were you there when that guy got his head stuck in the fish bowl? Holy shit, that was rich."

Was I there? I was tempted to ask.

"Hey." Frank tapped the top of a twelve-pack. "Didn't know you knew the Zod."

The Zod. I faked a grin. "Yeah, we go back a bit."

Frank nodded. "That's cool, that's cool."

No, it wasn't. And I was hoping that now we were all even, Zod would go back to pretending I didn't exist, forgetting who ratted him out to the police, forgetting everything about the kid who got him sent to jail.

"So, anyway," Frank said, "how much?"

"How much what?"

Frank laughed. "The beer. How much?"

"Oh, right," I said, skipping the ID check, the whole badass clerk thing feeling stupid now. I punched the keys, hit TOTAL. "With tax it's . . . nineteen fifty-eight."

Frank dug in his front pocket and took out a tightly wound roll of bills. He peeled two twenties off the top. "A pack of Kools too."

I rang it up, gave him back his change. Frank dropped the coins in the Save the Children jar, folded over the bills, and slid them into his shirt pocket, balancing the cigarettes on the top of a twelve-pack as he lifted them off the counter. "You and Zod hitting the Mirage tonight?"

The Mirage.

Mirror balls on the ceiling, flashing lights on the floor, a line fifty-people deep to get in every night. *"The hottest disco in town!"* At least that's what the commercials on the radio said. I'd never been there, never wanted to go anywhere near it, with or without Zod. But then why did I hear myself saying, "Yeah, maybe"?

"I'll keep an eye out for you," Frank said, backing toward the door. "And, hey. Merry Christmas."

I just sorta waved, not sure anymore what to say.

I DIDN'T HEAR her come in. But when I looked up from the *Rolling Stone* I was reading at the counter, there she was.

"So, we meet again," Dawn said.

I felt my heart jump, felt myself grinning like an idiot.

She looked out the front window at the swirling snow. "It's Christmas Eve. I figured you'd be closed by now."

"This ain't no wimpy 7-Eleven," I said. "We hang tough till midnight."

Dawn set her leather purse on the counter, flicked the melting snow out of her hair. "I was surprised to see you at Reggie's house the other day."

"I was surprised to see myself there too."

"Did Stevie — sorry — did *Zod* ever pay up?"

"In a way, I suppose."

"Let me guess," she said. "He paid you in drugs."

"Yeah . . ." I said, drawing it out like it was a question.

"That's because he knows you."

"If he knew me," I said, "he'd know I don't do drugs."

"Exactly," she said, and then waited for me to catch up. She unwrapped a stick of gum as I worked through it.

It took a moment, but I got there. "He knew I wouldn't take it."

"Yup. That's why he gave it to you."

"Then why go through all the bullshit?"

Dawn put the gum in her mouth, reached over the counter, and tossed the wrapper in the trash. "I'm still trying to figure that one out."

"You think there was something to it? The whole thing with the bet and the payoff?"

She smiled. "And you don't?"

The back room doors flung open with a squeaky thump, and George pushed a loaded shopping cart down the main aisle. "Break time's over, kid. Santa's got some soup cans for you to stock."

Dawn glanced at George, then back at me. "What time do you get outta here?"

I checked the clock. "Thirty minutes."

She looked down at her purse, gave a little shrug. "Wanna . . . I don't know . . . do something?"

"Like what?"

She sighed, and for a second I thought she looked nervous. "Maybe check out a midnight movie?"

It was Christmas Eve, I'd worked the last six hours, had all of fourteen dollars on me, and I barely knew this girl. Plus there was that whole psycho coke-fiend boyfriend thing.

There was only one possible answer.

I said, "Yeah, that'd be cool."

Dawn looked up and smiled.

"Hey," George shouted across the store. "These soup cans ain't gonna stack themselves."

I kept my eyes on hers. "What do you want to see?"

She laughed. "If I tell you, you won't go."

"*Saturday Night Fever,* right?"

Dawn squeezed her lips tight, turning an invisible key at the corner of her mouth.

"Gosh," I said, hamming it up. "I guess there's only one way I'm *ever* gonna find out."

She slung her purse onto her shoulder. "See you at midnight."

I watched her brush the snow off the windshield of a battered blue and white VW Beetle and drive out of the parking lot, "Hark! The Herald Angels Sing" drowning out whatever George was saying.

"ADMIT IT," SHE said. "You liked it."

It was two hours of disco, silly clothes, and dancing. Pure poly heaven. I was hard-wired to hate it. But — what do you know — I liked it. There was no way I was going to admit it, but I liked it.

"It was a lot darker than I thought it was gonna be," I said.

"What were you expecting, a comedy?"

"Well, I wasn't expecting a gang rape and a suicide, that's for sure."

“Yeah,” Dawn said, and after a pause, she added, “that part was a little too realistic for me.”

She pulled out of the mall parking lot and onto the main road. The snow had stopped while we were in the movie, and the plows had cleared the roads down to asphalt. A town truck went by going the other way, spraying her VW with salt. Karla usually freaked when that happened. Dawn didn’t seem to notice.

“That guy in the movie,” I said. “The one Travolta played?”

“Tony?”

“I can’t believe how his family treated the brother just because he didn’t want to be a priest.”

“All families are screwed up,” she said. “It’s sorta the definition.”

“Fits for mine,” I said. “I got two sisters. One younger, one older. Right there tells you how crazy it is.”

“Careful, I’m a girl too, you know,” she said, as if I needed a reminder. “What makes it so crazy?”

“Eileen — she’s the oldest — married, got a couple of kids. They’re all right. Most of the time. But Eileen?” I shook my head thinking about it. “She’s just like my mother. Acts like she’s my mother too. Until she needs something. Then she’s all, ‘Oh, you’re my brother, you gotta help.’ It’s all drama with her. Always has been, and I don’t see it getting any better.”

Dawn nodded. "Okay, I'll give you that one."

"Then there's Gail." I took a deep breath, let it out as a sigh. "She's younger than me, but she's done a lot more crazy shit than I ever have. She's not at home anymore."

"In jail?"

"No. She might *say* she is. My parents couldn't deal with her, so they sent her to live with my aunt and uncle in Vermont. I don't know, she might even like it there. It's a lot quieter at home, though. And a lot less interesting."

"Sounds like you miss her."

I smiled, remembering. "Me and Gail, the way we got along, you'd think we were ignoring each other. But it was just about giving space. We'd have these long talks. Not every day or anything, but you know what I mean. She's smart. Always has a book with her. Wouldn't know it from her grades, though. But that's because she was suspended all the time. More than me, even. Mostly because of her mouth. She cannot stand being told what to do. She sees things different and doesn't give a damn what anybody thinks about her."

Dawn nodded. "My kind of woman."

"Yeah, Gail's okay," I said. "Crazy, but okay."

"I got a younger sister too." She laughed softly. "I guess you could say she's crazy."

"As crazy as you?"

"No. Regular crazy. Technically she's mentally retarded, but the way some people treat her . . ."

"Oh," I said, sounding as stupid as I felt.

"She's the best person I know. She's this big, goofy bundle of love. Like it's the only thing she knows. Unless she's in a mood, then watch out. But she can't help herself. Unlike *most* people I know."

I assumed she meant Reg, but there could be dozens more people in her life that were the same way. There was no way for me to know. All I could do was make sure I wasn't one of them.

Dawn looked over at me, smiled. "*Any*way . . . the movie. What'd you think of the music?"

"Are you serious? It sucked."

"I liked it. It made the movie better."

"If by *better* you mean more depressing, then you're right." I turned in my seat to lean against the passenger door. "How would you have ended it?"

"What, the movie?"

"Yeah, if you were directing it, what would you have done with the ending?"

She shook her head slowly. "I wouldn't change a thing."

"I would. First, I'd get rid of the music, then I'd give it a happy ending."

She faked a shudder. "That would ruin it."

"What have you got against happy endings?"

"That's what we all want, isn't it? A story with a happy ending."

"What's wrong with that?"

Dawn laughed. "Absolutely nothing. But good luck getting one."

SUNDAY, DECEMBER 25

I PRIED OPEN AN EYE IN THE DIRECTION OF THE CLOCK: 9:45.

Back when we were kids, me and Gail and Eileen would have been up hours ago, tearing into the mound of presents. By seven a.m., there'd be nothing left to unwrap, and every battery in the house would have been rounded up to power my Major Matt Mason Space Crawler or a Barbie Dune Buggy. It was noisy and hectic and hot, and it would only get worse—or better, if you were a kid—when our grandparents dropped by with their armload of presents.

That was forever ago. Long before Eileen got pregnant and Gail got her attitude. Now it was just me and my parents, and they'd be leaving for Eileen's soon, bringing a carload of toys for the grandkids. If my parents timed it right, Gail would call from Vermont when they were at Eileen's. That way they could spread the call around the three of them, none of them wanting to have to talk with her for too long. I could've used a long talk with Gail, but I'd have to miss it.

I was scheduled to work from one p.m. till closing. Eleven glorious time-and-a-half hours. It took a lot of sucking up, but it was worth it, since it bought me the kind of valid excuse that would get me out of spending the day trapped at my sister's, watching the football game with our parents, her in-laws, and other assorted strangers. If it was just the kids, I'd go. It'd be fun watching them play with all the toys, letting them beat me at Sorry! or whatever game they'd be getting. And it was Christmas, so they'd be on their best behavior. I couldn't say that about anyone else who'd be there.

Stretched out in my bed, I thought about Dawn.

She'd dropped me off after two, not even a hint of a possible good-night kiss, both of us playing it straight platonic, some vague lines about it being fun and doing it again sometime, everything cool until she said, "And whatever you do, don't tell *anybody* I went to the movies with you." That's when Reg popped back in my head, all coked-up and beady-eyed, looking for a reason to cut some punk kid's throat.

Over *Saturday Night Fever* of all things.

And I didn't even get any. Well, it wasn't like it was the first time *that* had happened. Or didn't happen.

Besides, she had a boyfriend. He was older, and he had money and his own place, and even though he was bat-shit crazy and a dealer, I knew that I had zero chance with her. I had a good chance, however, of getting my ass kicked *because* of her. Still, as I climbed out of bed and headed for the bathroom, I knew it was the best Saturday night I'd had in a long while.

Five minutes later, I took my usual seat across from my

mom at the kitchen table. My father was at the sink, rinsing out his TAKE THIS JOB AND SHOVE IT! coffee mug. "So, you finally decided to get outta bed, huh?"

Obviously, I thought, mumbling something that could pass for a greeting.

"A Merry Christmas to you, too," my mother said, her smile telling me how to play it.

"Merry Christmas, Mom," I said, saying it like I knew I should. "You too, Dad."

He grunted. "Coffee?"

"Yeah, sure. Thanks." There was no reason not to be polite. It was Christmas, after all. It was the least I could do, since I hadn't gotten them anything.

My mother lit a cigarette, her fourth that morning by the look of the ashtray. "You bump into Santa when you rolled in last night?"

It wasn't funny, but I chuckled on cue. It had only taken a second to read their mood—light, TV family-ish, a hint of that when-I-was-your-age nostalgia mixed with a heavy dose of artificial holiday spirit. It was a rare mood, easily shattered, so I went along, sticking to the aw-shucks response I knew they were looking for.

"Whoever dropped you off needs to learn some manners," my father said. "What's he doing beeping like that at two in the morning?"

"Got me," I said, pausing, then adding, "But next time I see her, I'll ask."

That got the raised-eyebrow reaction I knew it would, my parents glancing at each other, their little boy growing up so fast. My mother puffed on her Winston. "So, is this a girl from your school?"

"No, she graduated last year," I said, assuming it was close to the truth. "We caught a late movie."

They shared another knowing glance while I made a golly-gee face. It all felt silly, but they seemed to like it.

My father passed me a cup of black coffee, then my mother handed me an envelope. "This is from both of us and . . . well, you'll see. Merry Christmas."

This was new.

We were past sitting on the floor and opening presents as a family, but my mom was still big on gifts for Christmas. Cash was for birthdays and graduations — if you got that far — but not Christmas. Then it was store bought and wrapped with a bow, just like the ads showed. I gave a puzzled smile and pretended to weigh the envelope. A card, hopefully with something inside. "Is it a new coat?"

"Just open it, smartass," my father said, leaning over the counter to watch.

I tore open the envelope and slid the card out. There was a cartoon elf on the front, so it wasn't going to be the sappy poem kind, thank god. I took a quick sip of hot coffee and read the front of the card out loud.

"'According to Santa, you're on the nice list this year. And you know what that means.'" I opened the card, and a piece of notepaper fluttered out onto my lap. I finished reading. "'It means Santa's on the sauce again. Merry Christmas, love, Mom and Dad.'" I looked up at both of them and smiled. "Ha-ha, very funny."

"Read that paper," my mother said, gesturing with her cigarette.

It was single sheet from the pad by the phone, folded once in the middle. Inside it said "Reg/insurance."

They knew? No way. I read it again, staring at the words. *No frickin' way.*

"He doesn't get it," my mother said. "I told you to be more specific."

"Just give him a second," my father said. "He'll get it."

They *couldn't* know. Could they? No, it had to mean something else. This Reg couldn't be *that* Reg. The pressure on, I took a guess. "You're gonna get me regular insurance to drive your car?"

"Not *my* car," my father said, and from across the counter he tossed me a set of keys. "Your car."

I looked at the keys—something familiar about them—then I leaned forward to look out the front window to the driveway.

My mother said, "Check the garage."

"You kidding?"

"Go look."

I slid my chair back, walked past the fridge, and down the step to the closed-in porch that led to the garage. I put a hand on the doorknob, then turned to look back, half expecting them to bust out laughing.

"Come on, we haven't got all day," my father said.

I opened the door. Parked in the garage, a small red bow on the windshield, was Karla's green 1973 Ford Pinto.

"She wanted you to have it," my mother said.

My father laughed. "Since the junkyard wouldn't take it."

"Oh, stop. It's still a good car, and Nick knows it better than anybody else."

I ran a hand through my hair.

"That paper is your Christmas present from us," my father said. "We'll pay for the registration and the first six months of insurance. After that, you're on your own. The maintenance and gas, too. That's all up to you, starting right now. And I'm warning you, I don't want a broken-down car in the driveway. That happens, I'll have it towed outta here."

"And no drinking and driving, either," my mother said. "And if you get so much as a parking ticket . . ."

There was more, but I couldn't hear it, my other senses shutting down so I could focus on the car.

It was all rusted along the bottom of the doors, the one

bumper drooped, the muffler was going, the passenger window was cracked, there were two flat tires in the trunk, and no jack. And a skipping eight-track player. I used to tell Karla that it was a piece of shit on wheels. It was still a piece of shit. But now it was mine. My cheeks were burning from grinning so hard.

Maybe Karla was right after all.

Maybe this was going to be the best year ever.

"IT MUST SUCK to have to work Christmas."

"It's not bad," I said, ringing up the gallon of milk and pound of coffee the man had on the counter. "There's not a lot to do, and I get paid time and a half."

"Time-and-a-half of shit is still shit," the man said. He was older, balding, thin except for the bowling-ball beer belly that made him look seven months pregnant. "What's that work out to, like six bucks an hour?" He shook his head as he stuffed the change in his pants pocket, dropping two cents in the need-a-penny-take-a-penny dish, then heading out into the dark night.

I knew exactly how much it worked out to.

$3.97 an hour.

And I'd already figured out how much I'd make for the twenty hours I'd be putting in that weekend.

$63.52 after taxes, give or take a dime.

Not a lot, but more than I'd normally get. Enough for gas,

inspection, a couple eight-tracks, and one of those air fresheners I could hang on the rearview mirror long enough to get rid of the cigarette smell. I'd only had the car for twelve hours and could already see where my money would be going.

Technically it was still Karla's car. And technically, I shouldn't be driving it. It was still in her name and under her insurance. *If* she hadn't canceled the policy already. She was on the road with what's-his-name and didn't leave a number where she could be reached in Florida once she got there. Her mother might know about the insurance, but there was also a chance that she didn't know about Karla giving the car away. Better not to ask.

I assumed my parents knew all this, but they let me drive anyway. Odds were I wouldn't hit something or do anything that would attract the attention of the police. Not on the first day, at any rate. And if I could drive myself, there was no need for my parents to pick me up or to pretend that they felt bad about me having to walk home at midnight.

With George in the back room, I spent some of my Christmas night in front of the store's small display of automotive products, sniffing the plastic wrappers on dangling car air fresheners.

At quarter to twelve, George went out and started his car. He brushed the snow off the windshield, cranked the defroster, and left the car idling, ensuring a quick and warm getaway at closing time. When midnight arrived, he turned off the store lights, locked the front door, and bolted, leaving me alone in the snowy parking lot.

It was fluffy snow, the kind that kicked up when you walked through it. I pulled the sleeve of my coat over my hand and cleared the windshield of my car with my arm before I thought to look inside for a snow brush. I was reaching for the door handle when I noticed that someone was crouched down in the back seat.

I stepped back quickly, my stomach flipping while a hot charge raced up my spine, part fear, part anger. I punched the passenger window. "Get the hell outta my car!"

The shape moved—slow, cautious—and I tensed up, balancing my weight, getting ready for a fight. I could hear the handle being pulled, and when the door cracked open, the dome light went on and I saw the blood.

"I'm sorry," Dawn said. "I didn't know where else to go. And I didn't want to go in the store with that guy there. I figured this was your car, and it was unlocked, so . . ."

Her cheek looked puffy and red, and there was dried blood on her face, in her hair, on the charcoal-gray scarf she had used as a bandage. Her left eye was dark, and I couldn't tell if it was a rising bruise or running makeup. And I didn't know what to do.

"Oh my god, are you okay?"

She managed a smile. "I've been worse."

"What happened? Were you in an accident?"

"An accident?" She touched her cheek with her fingers. "I guess you could call it that."

I looked around, but there was no one to help. "Can I get you to the hospital?"

She shook her head. "I'm cold. Can you turn on the car?"

I started the car and cranked the heat, then helped Dawn around front to the passenger side before climbing back behind the wheel.

"I can take you to the hospital—"

"No, please," she said, sliding down low in the seat. "I'll be okay. Promise."

I put the car in drive and pulled closer to the front of the store, the night lights spilling into the car. I looked at her and she looked away. "Who did this to you?"

"Can you just drive? Please?"

So I drove.

Down past the school, past the park, sticking to the side roads, the ones without streetlights and traffic. I kept both hands on the wheel, eyes on the road, radio off, the way Karla had liked me to drive when she was upset.

I drove below the speed limit, signaling all of my turns even though I was the only car on the road.

I drove because I didn't know what else to do.

We'd been driving for close to thirty minutes when she reached over and turned down the heat.

"Thanks," I said. "I was starting to roast."

"It's your car. You could've turned it off anytime."

"I wanted you to be comfortable."

Out of the corner of my eye, I could see her looking at me, watching me as I drove. I wondered what she saw.

I kept driving, and she kept looking. Then she said, "You're gonna use up all your gas."

"Just filled it today. It hasn't even dipped below the F yet."

"I didn't know what to do, Nick."

I swallowed. "That's okay. I don't mind."

"He had yelled a lot before, and he, you know, shoved me and stuff. And I'd seen him slap other girls. But never me." She tilted her head back, looked up at the roof of the car. "God, that sounds awful, doesn't it?"

It did, but I said nothing.

"I mean, I've been there, *right in the room,* when he and Cory beat the hell out of guys. Mostly ones who owed them money. But there were others who just . . ." She closed her eyes and held her breath a long time, letting it out in short bursts. "I don't want to live like this anymore."

I cleared my throat, not sure of what to say, but I knew I had to say something. "It's not too late to change."

"Change what?"

"Everything. How you live, what you do. You can change it all. I know it."

Eyes still closed, she smiled.

"Really," I said, positive that I was right. "Just pick something and do it. Start with moving out of there. Can't you move in with friends?"

She chuckled. "Supposedly, they *are* my friends."

"You don't have any others?"

Dawn rolled her head to the side and looked at me. "Well, there's you."

My eyes widened.

"Don't worry," she said, the laugh still in her voice. "I'm not going to follow you home."

"What about family?"

Big sigh. "That's why I'm living where I'm living."

A pickup truck flew by in the other lane. The headlights filled the car as it went past, then the truck was gone and the night seemed darker.

"I needed money for my sister," Dawn said. "And Reg had it. So I moved in with him." Another sigh. "I told you about Terri. She's got some weird health problems. A *lot* of 'em for a twelve-year-old. And mentally she's . . . well, you know."

I didn't know—how could I?—but I tried to understand.

"I'd do anything for her." She kept her head down and picked at a loose thread on the end of her scarf. "Whenever

I think I've got it hard, that things aren't going my way, I think about Terri. Puts it in perspective."

There was more to the story about her sister, but I sensed that was all she was going to share. "You still got options," I said. "There's lots of shelters—"

"For homeless people? No, thanks. I got myself into this, and I'll find a way out." She pointed down the road. "Take a left at the stop sign. That'll get you to the expressway."

I looked at her, at the caked blood in her hair, on her eyebrow, her puffy cheek, her soft, red lips. "You're going back there?"

"It'll be all right."

"You don't know that."

"Yes, I do," she said. "They will have left for Cleveland by now. Picking up a shipment. I'll have the place to myself for a while." She looked at me and smiled. "And no, you can't come in."

I smiled too. "I wasn't gonna ask."

"Well, I'm glad," she said, turning on the radio, flicking it over to the R&B station. "For now."

MONDAY, DECEMBER 26

It was after ten when I woke up.

My father had left for work hours ago, and there was a note from my mom saying she and Eileen were out post-Christmas shopping, so I had the house to myself. I put an album on the stereo — *Queens of Noise* — cranked up the volume, took a long, hot shower, and thought about Dawn.

She had me drop her off down the street from Reg's house and told me not to hang around, but I stayed there until she got in the front door, waiting for yelling or a scream for help. It was quiet, though, and after ten minutes I went home.

It didn't make sense, Dawn going back to that house, not just walking away. I couldn't see Karla putting up with it, and Karla wasn't nearly as tough as Dawn. But then again, Karla didn't have a mentally retarded sister counting on her. That's why Dawn went back. And that said a lot about her.

Dawn was smart, that was obvious, and not just street-smart, either. Something in the way she talked, the way she looked at me, her dark eyes taking everything in, seeing everything clearer, deeper.

Maybe it was because she was older.

Wait, was she?

She could be twenty-five for all I knew.

Or sixteen.

Girls with that look, they could pass for whatever age they needed to.

Still, she'd be old enough to know that it wasn't going to get any better staying with Reg, and smart enough to know she needed a way out. But there she was, going back, not a word about moving on. None of it made sense.

Like her being out by the Stop-N-Go at midnight.

I had a lot to think about.

I SPENT A good hunk of the afternoon trying to get the car registered at the Department of Motor Vehicles.

I waited in lines, filled out forms, waited in different lines with different forms, only to be told that they couldn't do anything without NYDMV 3237-C(a), the one form that Karla had to sign. I explained why that was impossible, they explained why they didn't care, in the end letting me know that given the estimated value of the car — $50 — and the cost of registration — $31.75 — no one would be checking the signatures. But just to be safe, I used two different pens.

At three thirty, I screwed on the new license plates and headed home.

I was running on four hours of restless sleep, so when I got there, I crashed on my bed till dinner. It was just me and my mother — my father *working late again* — so we went with cereal like we usually did when he wasn't around. I watched the tail end of the national news, then ancient black-and-white reruns of *The Munsters* and *The Addams Family* before falling asleep on the couch. My mother woke me again at ten. I went up to my room, put on my headphones, and listened to music, nodding off around midnight.

Then there I was, in Reg's house.

The black guy was there too. Cory. That was his name. He was there, shuffling decks of cards. Table covered with cards. Dawn was there. Blood on her face again, but I couldn't see a cut. She didn't notice anyway, too busy flipping over the cards in front of her, every one of them a red queen. She looked up and smiled and said something, something that sounded important, but I couldn't make out the words. And there was a hole in the wall, and it got bigger, so I stepped through it and I was in the living room of my house, and my father was on the couch, watching a football game on TV, only it looked more like baseball, and there was a woman on the couch with him. I couldn't see her face, but I knew it was the one in the car that night at the Stop-N-Go. Then my mother came on the TV and said, "Your father has to work late tonight," and the channel changed and it was the aisle at work, and Zod was walking toward me and there was a knife, and we were in the parking lot again and it was dark, and Zod stuck the knife clean through the guy's arm and then in the guy's stomach once, twice, and Dawn screamed and it was her with the knife, and I was bleeding now and, damn, there was blood everywhere, so much blood, while Karla drove away and Zod and Reg ran at me and Dawn smiled—and I sat up, soaked in sweat, my heart pounding, my breath choppy, the *hisssss* from the stereo at the end of the record loud in my ears.

WEDNESDAY, DECEMBER 28

DAYTIME TELEVISION SUCKED.

The major networks were all game shows and soap operas. The cable channels were no better, either showing different versions of the same things the networks had on or running old movies, interrupted every eight minutes for twenty minutes of commercials. There were stations that only showed commercials—and what was up with *two* stations showing school lunch menus from September?

Thirty-six channels and nothing on.

I flicked back through the cable box one last time, leaving it on *Let's Make a Deal*. It was stupid, but it was something.

The week between Christmas and New Year's used to be the best week of the year. No school—which right there made it great—and I had all this new stuff to play with, the tree was still up with the lights, there were tons of cookies left over, and I could stay in my pajamas all day, doing nothing but watching cartoons. It was pretty damn sweet.

It changed around the same time toys went from being the coolest things in the world to something I cleared out of my bedroom to make room for a stereo. The tree went next—no need to go through all that hassle for teenagers—and it was easier to buy a package of Oreos than mess up the kitchen making cookies. I couldn't sit around in my pajamas all day, since I didn't wear any, and *when* did the cartoons become so lame?

The contestants were bidding on a hot tub when the phone rang. At first I wasn't going to answer it—no one would be calling me—but it kept going, and after a dozen more rings, I picked it up, and Zod said, "I hear you got wheels."

I didn't remember giving Zod the number, but then I didn't remember much from that night. "Yeah, I got a car but—"

"Good. You remember Reg's place, over on Genesee Street?"

"Not really," I said, knowing exactly where it was.

"Yes, you do, shithead. By the closed gas station, down the street from that strip club all the brothers go to."

"I don't know. I wasn't paying attention," I said, then I heard three quick *thwacks*, the sound of a receiver being slammed against the side of a glass phone booth.

"You paying attention now?"

I took a breath, closed my eyes. "Okay, okay, I'm listening."

"Reg's house. One hour. *Don't* make us come get you."

I was able to say, "Wait, listen," before I heard the dial tone that told me Zod had hung up.

By the time I turned onto Genesee Street, I'd run through all my options six times each. There weren't that many to consider.

I could ignore Zod's call and his summons to Reg's house. It was the easiest answer, and it would send a clear message.

Any normal person would understand.

And that was the problem.

Zod would get the message, then he'd deliver one of his own. He knew where I lived, knew how to get in, and I had no doubt that Zod would pay a visit, probably when I was the only one at home, but you couldn't bet on that, either, not with a psycho.

I thought about explaining the situation to my parents. I could tell them that I was sorry, that I'd made a mistake or two, and now this guy from my past was back, and I didn't know what to do, and, boy, I really needed their help.

No way.

Their help had gotten me to a point in my life where I needed a list to get me out of it. You could say that it was the way they raised me that gave me the confidence I needed to reinvent myself, but I ain't buying it. Their hands-off parenting style wasn't part of some master plan to make us better adults. It was simply the least they had to do until we could fend for ourselves and get out of their hair. Maybe it was the way their parents raised them, I don't know, but I did know that asking them for help was something I wasn't going to do. Running drugs for Zod, sure. Running to Mommy and Daddy, no way. Pretty sad when you think about it.

So, no, my parents could *not* know.

For a second or two, I thought about telling Jay and Dan-O and the guys, see if they'd back me up, but I knew I wouldn't ask and that they'd only laugh if I did. We barely stood up for each other in the best of times. Now? They'd line up to see me get beat down.

Karla would've listened. She wouldn't have laughed or given me worthless advice. She probably would have told me what I knew already, but she would have listened.

Other options—like telling a teacher or calling one of those counseling lines—weren't worth the second it took to dismiss them.

I thought about my list. *Stand up* and *stand fast* seemed to fit the situation. Stand up to Zod and refuse to play his game, then stand fast to that decision. It's what the warlord of Bimskala would do. Then again, he had a sword and a laser pistol. And a princess.

I pulled up in front of Reg's house, still thinking about my list. Had following it brought me here, or would I have ended up here anyway, in a situation no list was going to get me out of?

It was deep in the winter afternoon, and the streetlights were already on. Somebody had busted out the bulb in the light in front of the house, making the walkway and porch that much darker. The flickering blue glow of the TV backlit the bed sheet that served as a curtain. I knocked just loud enough to be heard. A few seconds later the two deadbolts clicked back, the chain came off, and the door swung open.

Zod grinned. "I told you he'd show."

Someone shouted, "Shut the damn door. It's freezing out there." And then I was inside.

Cory was on the couch, one hand in a bag of potato chips, the other around a skinny blond chick, both of them snuggled up under a tartan blanket, watching a rerun of *Gilligan's Island.* At one end of the table was a pudgy lump with a weak mustache who kept his eyes glued to the TV across the room. At the other end sat a black guy, older than the rest, his Jheri curl glistening under the hanging lamp.

And there was Reg, cigarette in his mouth, arm flung across the back of the chair, looking right at me.

There was no sign of Dawn.

Zod slapped me on the shoulder, then strode past to take the last seat at the table, smiling like he knew what was coming.

I walked over, burying my hands in the pockets of my jean jacket so they wouldn't see them shake. I stood near Zod and kept the front door right behind me. The black guy gave me half a glance, then went back to the magazine he was reading. The pudgy guy stayed with the TV castaways.

I tried to keep my eyes on the center of the table, at the deck of cards that Dawn had dealt in my dream, but I could feel the stare, and when I looked up, Reg locked on and said, "What's this you gave Steve the snow?"

It didn't click at first, and I could feel my mouth slowly dropping open as my brain raced to translate *Steve* into *Zod*, *snow* into *cocaine*. I managed a faint "Yeah," then a second later, "I gave it to him."

Reg held my stare. "You don't trust my product?"

"No," I said, catching myself as I said it. "*I mean yes.* Yes, I . . . I trust it. The, uh, product."

"So why you giving it away?"

It was a simple question, the kind anybody with any sense would've asked. The answer? That wasn't so simple. And it wouldn't have made any sense to the guys at the table. But as I felt the sweat start to bead on my lip, and my knee began to twitch, the only answer I could think of was the wrong one. I heard myself say it anyway. "I'm not into drugs."

No reaction.

No snickering, no mumbled *bullshit*s.

Nothing.

I blinked, shuffled my feet. Reg kept staring.

"Your friends say you don't cut 'em any slack at the Stop-N-Go. Make 'em pay every time. Full price. Even a bag of ice. That true?"

Friends? I shrugged. "I guess."

"You *guess?*" Reg dropped an open hand on the table. "I don't want you *guessing.* Do you make your friends pay, yes or no?"

"Yes," I said. "They have to pay."

"But you don't pay, do you? You take whatever you want," Reg said, counting off on his fingers. "Beer. Cigarettes. *Ice.*"

The black guy chuckled at that, but Reg's expression didn't change.

"No, I don't take anything."

"You take money from the till, though, right? Ten bucks here, twenty there . . ."

"No," I said. "Nothing."

"Not even once?"

"No. Never."

Reg slapped the table — hard this time — and leaned forward, his eyes on fire. "Why the hell not?"

The room was quiet. I realized that the TV was off, nobody moving, all of them watching me, waiting.

"Do you think you'll get caught? Is *that* why you don't steal?"

I wet my lips, swallowed, shook my head. What did they want me to say?

The short lumpy guy turned. "The man asked you a quest—"

Reg's arm swung up, catching the guy on the cheek, rocking his head back, Reg never taking his eyes off me. "I'm gonna ask you *one more time,*" Reg said. "*Why* don't you steal from that *shithole store?*"

I tried, but there was nothing in my head but the stupid, lame, pansy-ass truth. I cleared my throat and said, "It doesn't belong to me."

"Excuse me?"

"I said it doesn't belong to me."

"So just because it doesn't *belong to you,*" Reg said, the others all laughing at his imitation of my mumbling, "you think you shouldn't take any of it."

"Yeah."

"And because *you* don't steal, you don't let *anybody else* steal either, is that right?"

"That's right," I said, quicker now, guessing that it didn't matter anymore.

Reg narrowed his eyes. "You telling me *I* come in that store, *I* steal something, *you're* gonna stop me?"

Silence.

Time stopping.

And in that silence, in that frozen moment, a realization.

They were all holding their breath.

They were waiting.

Not for Reg.

For me.

Waiting for me to break.

I didn't know what would happen next, but in that instant I realized it was time to stand up.

"Hey, shithead," Reg said. "I asked you if you think you would—"

"Yes," I said. "I'd stop you."

Reg smirked. "Just how *you* gonna stop *me* from taking what I want?"

"I don't know," I said. "But I would."

All eyes were on Reg now as he leaned back in the chair.

Then he laughed.

They all laughed.

Not at me.

With me.

"I told you," Zod said.

"We'll see," Reg said, still smiling, still looking at me. "Get this kid a chair. We're gonna have a talk."

THURSDAY, DECEMBER 29

I HATED GOING IN THE STORE WHEN I WASN'T WORKING. Any unpaid seconds in the place felt like punishment. But Thursday was payday and Saturday was New Year's Eve, and I didn't want to be caught short on cash for any of it, even if my only plan was not being home at midnight.

Jay's parents always went out of town for New Year's, so there'd be a blow-out party at his house. Last year they went through a half pound of weed, twenty cases of beer, and a big bottle of Wild Turkey that I helped kill. Months later, just the thought of doing shots made me nauseous. This year there'd be more of everything, but I'd sit alone in my own driveway, sipping hot chocolate at midnight, before I'd show up at Jay's.

The road was clear and the potholes were easy to see. There were too many to avoid, but at least I could pick the ones I'd hit, keeping the frame-shaking, eight-track-popping jolts to a minimum. The car didn't drift to the right like it did when Karla drove it, so there was no need for sudden jerks of the wheel, and the muffler was making some noise, but that was easily fixed by cranking up the stereo. It was the Ramones—I taped the album over an old Genesis eight-track—and it was loud and hard and fast and exactly what I needed to wake up my morning.

I pulled into the parking lot and took a spot near the door. Employees were supposed to park at the far end of the lot, saving the close spaces for customers, but I wasn't there to work, and Penelope was so happy to see me, she wouldn't have cared if I parked sideways in the lone handicapped spot.

"Look who came to visit," Penelope said, scurrying out from behind the counter, standing on her toes to give me a hug. "How's my favorite stock boy?"

"Stock *man,*" I said, hugging back.

It was impossible not to like Penelope Robinson. She was everyone's grandmother, cool aunt, and favorite teacher, all in one pint-size package. I only saw her on the rare times our shifts bumped together, but she still treated me like her favorite person in the whole world, just like she treated most people who came in the door.

"I know you're not going to break my heart and tell me you're only here for your check."

I overacted a shocked expression. "You mean it's *payday? Already?*"

"Don't get too excited, stock man. There's no holiday money in that check. Only straight pay, no time-and-a-half." She stepped back behind the counter and popped open the register, lifted out the cash drawer with one hand, and took out a thin stack of white envelopes with the other, handing them to me. "Yours is near the top."

I took the envelope with my name on it and gave her back the rest. Inside there'd be a check for $24.77. Less than the street value of the short line of coke Reg had snorted off the tabletop.

"So tell me," Penelope said, pinching my arm as she said it. "Who is this raven-haired beauty who came looking for your phone number?"

My head snapped up.

"Oh, so you *do* know her," she said. "Pretty, in a tough kind of way. Looks like that biker girl on *Happy Days*."

I stuffed the envelope in my jeans, trying hard to play it smooth. "What'd she say?"

"What do you think she said? She wanted your phone number."

"Did you give it to her?"

Penelope shook her head and made that *tsk*-ing sound. "Now, Nicky, you know very well the rules don't allow us to share any personal information with customers. Even attractive ones."

"So you didn't give it to her?"

"I'm sorry, dear. Mr. Starks was standing right here, and you know what he would have done if he saw me going through the employee phone list with a customer."

I looked up at the ceiling. I didn't think I could ever be

pissed at Penelope, but I felt it coming. I closed my eyes and started counting.

"The rules are very clear about giving out phone numbers," she was saying. "Funny, though, they don't say anything at all about *getting* phone numbers."

I opened my eyes and there was Penelope, waving a folded slip of paper between two tiny fingers.

I STUCK A STRAW in my Pepsi and watched as Dawn emptied a fourth pack of sugar and a third creamer into the small Buckman's Donuts mug. "You told me you liked coffee," I said.

"I do."

"How can you taste it with all the other stuff in there?"

"I like my coffee like I like my men," she said. "Hot, sweet, and tan." She reached over and pushed up the sleeve of my sweatshirt, my pale, winter skin looking whiter against the black fabric. She smiled at me. "Well, two outta three . . ."

I waited a moment, just in case she wanted to say more, but she didn't, so I said, "I suppose you heard all about my little meeting with King Reg."

"I heard their side of it. Tell me yours."

I shrugged. "Got a call from Zod—"

"Aka Little Stevie Zodarecky."

"—and he said Reg wanted to see me. So I went. They were all sitting around—"

"Who?"

"Zod . . . or Steve. Whatever. Reg, of course. Cory. Some blond chick—"

"Charlene," Dawn said, trying and failing to capture a Texas drawl. "She works at the Klassy Kat. It was love at first pole dance." She sipped at her coffee. "Was Lester there?"

"Brother with the Jheri curl? Yeah, he was there. Didn't say much."

"He never does."

"Oh, and there was another guy. White, short, looks like he's trying to grow a mustache?"

Dawn made a face. "Freddie. He's the runner."

"Him?"

"Not *running* runner," she said, a laugh in her voice. "He's like an errand boy. He picks up the goods or drops off the cash. Keeps Reg one step removed from the actual deal."

"He looked a little . . ."

"Pathetic? Weak? Ball-less?"

I smiled. "Yeah. One of those."

"He is," she said. "That's why they picked him. They think he's a wuss, so he'll never try anything stupid. I don't trust the guy. I think that whole thing is an act. But Reg thinks he's okay, so it doesn't matter what anybody else thinks. Freddie hasn't pocketed anything yet. But, oh boy, if he ever did . . ." She shook her head and went back to her coffee.

I thought about Freddie, the dull look in his eyes as he

watched *Gilligan's Island,* Reg smacking his face for talking out of turn, how the guy just took it, backing down like a nervous puppy. It didn't seem like an act to me.

"Anyway," Dawn said. "How did Reg bring it up?"

"He started asking me about my job—was it true I didn't steal stuff, that I wouldn't let my friends steal anything."

"You let me get away."

"We weren't friends then."

She grinned. "Go on."

"Then he says, 'What if *I* tried to steal something?' and I told him I'd have to stop him. Or try to, anyway."

"I'm *sure* he liked that."

"It's funny, I think he did." I stabbed the straw through the ice to the bottom of the glass. "That's when he offered me a job."

"What kind of job?"

"He didn't say. Just said he was looking for someone he could trust."

Dawn added another packet of sugar to her coffee, stirring it in as she thought.

"Maybe he's looking for somebody to sell at my school," I said.

"No, Steve handles that stuff. And people below his level never meet Reg. He thinks it'll protect him if one of them gets busted."

"Would it?"

"Probably. It'll take a lot more than a nickel-bag sale to get him locked up."

I looked at her. "You sound disappointed?"

Her smile twitched. She drew in a deep breath, paused, started to say something, and stopped. She took a sip of her coffee and propped her chin in her hand. "Anyway, this job offer. They said you're thinking it over."

I shook my head. "I told them I didn't want anything to do with them or their drugs or their money, and that they should leave me alone and stay the hell away."

"You *said* that?"

"Not those words, no. But they got the idea."

"No, they didn't. What *they* heard was that you're thinking it over."

"Well, I'm not, so they can forget it."

"They won't," Dawn said. "Once they get an idea in their little heads, they don't let it go. And right now, that idea is that you're going to be working for Reg."

"And if I say no?"

"They'll hear yes."

"I guess I'll worry about that when it happens," I said, knowing that I was already worrying about it.

"That's what I said." She took a pack of Virginia Slims from her purse and pulled a cigarette out with her lips. "Then it happened."

"You *work* for him?"

She sparked a BIC lighter and lit the cigarette, took a long drag. "I told you, I needed money. Well, technically Terri needed the money, and since my mother never did the paperwork and since it wasn't 'critical' or 'covered,' and because 'Rules are rules' and 'We can't make an exception,' I needed eighteen hundred upfront, fast. Who's got money like that laying around? A friend of a friend introduced me to Reg. I was going to do his books, keep track of the money. No drugs, not even the cash, just the accounting. He paid good, I'll give him that. Then the job changed. Now Lester gets paid for doing the books. And I get paid for doing Reg."

I kept my eyes on my Pepsi, but I could feel her looking at me.

"I know what that makes me," she said. "And I don't care. I'd do worse things than that for my sister."

She took another drag of her cigarette. I felt she was going to say more, but then the waitress was there with the cheery how's-everybody-doing-can-I-freshen-up-your-drinks bit, leaving behind a stack of sugar packets and a pile of creamers, and the moment passed. When Dawn was done diluting her coffee, she slid down in her seat, sipping from the mug. It was a simple move—awkward, really—and not the kind of thing that was supposed to be attractive.

But it was.

I wanted to tell her that.

And I wanted to tell her that I didn't care about Reg, or what she was doing, or what others might think.

And I wanted to tell her about my list, show her the copy I kept folded in my wallet, explain what each line meant and why they were important to me. I wanted to tell her that I admired her courage, that I respected her decisions, no matter how bad they seemed. And, most of all, I wanted to tell her that from that second on, I would be there for her, through anything that came our way. But before I could say any of it, Dawn asked, "What are you doing New Year's Eve?"

I sighed. "Working till midnight at the Stop-N-Go. Then, who knows. You?"

She tapped her cigarette in the ashtray. "What I want to do is get all dressed up, go out to dinner someplace nice. The Rio Bamba, maybe. Or Top of the Plaza. I want to dance and drink champagne at midnight, and stay up to watch the sunrise at the beach and go for breakfast, still wearing my dress."

"I'm not big on dancing," I said. "The rest sounds good, though."

She took a drag. "I won't be doing any of it. Staying up, maybe, but that's only because Reg and company will be making so much noise I won't be able to sleep. It'll be cold pizza and beer as they sit around getting stoned, watching the stupid ball drop." She looked away. I watched the smoke from her cigarette twist toward the ceiling fan. Without turning her head and in a voice just loud enough to hear, she said, "I need a new life."

I OPENED THE front door of the house and they were on me, their tiny arms tangling up my legs, their high-pitched squeals of "Uncle Nick" making my ears ring.

Connie was the oldest—five or six, something like that—but Jodi had the tighter grip, holding on to my knee and riding my leg like a swing. Connie looked like her dad, squinty eyes and square jaw, and Jodi was the mini-version of her mother, with the same high cheeks and turned-up nose, and that same I-deserve-it attitude that usually got her what she wanted. I liked it when they visited, but I loved it when they went home. They were cute and all that, but they were exhausting, and when they got tired and cranky, there was nothing cute about them.

If Connie and Jodi were there, so was Eileen.

I spent a few minutes pretending to be interested in Dancerella, then a few more than I thought would be necessary to lose a game of Hungry Hungry Hippos before making my way to the kitchen. My mother was at her normal spot at the table, facing my way but looking past me. Eileen was sitting where she sat when she was a kid. Her eyes were red and she didn't smile. There was a cloud of blue smoke above them, a smoldering ashtray filled with butts on the table, and a suitcase on the floor. I opened the refrigerator and looked inside. I didn't want anything, but I still looked. Better than hearing what I knew was coming.

My mother motioned with her cigarette. "Go get the girls' things out of the back of your sister's car."

I shook the milk carton to see if there was enough to dunk some cookies. There wasn't.

My mother drummed her fingers on the table. "*Nicholas.*"

"I heard you," I said. I shut the fridge, walked over, and leaned on the counter. I looked at my sister. She had dark circles under her eyes, the kind that come with age and lack of sleep, and there were a few gray hairs among the dark roots in her dirty blond hair. An hour a day under a sun-lamp gave her skin a leathery tan. It was hard to believe she was only twenty-three. "You want the bags in your old room?"

They exchanged a glance.

Of course they wouldn't go in her room.

She'd "need her space."

Just like last time.

And they wouldn't go in Gail's old room, since my mother had spent the year turning it into her sewing center. It didn't matter that she didn't sew — that room was not an option.

That left one place.

"Put them on the floor in your room for now," my mother said.

I knew that "For now" meant "For as long as they're here."

It also meant I'd be back in the basement, on the army cot they had bought the first time Eileen had moved out on her husband. That was two years ago. It was a wet spring that year, and every time it rained, water would roll down the cinderblock walls of our unfinished basement. It was winter now, so the basement would be dry. It'd be cold and the cot would still be too short and uncomfortable, and there'd be even more junk down there than before. But at least my clothes wouldn't smell like mildew.

"I *really* appreciate this," Eileen said. "Me and Allen just need a little time apart, that's all."

Just like last time.

I was about to say something smartass, something that was more cruel than clever, when I remembered item number three on my list. Like it or not, she was my sister, and as much as I *didn't* like it, I needed to stand by her.

"My room's not as big as you think," I said. "Let me move some stuff to the basement first."

It's not what I wanted to do, but if that list was going to mean anything, it's what I had to do.

I HEARD THE phone ring above me.

The kitchen chair scraped against the floor, and my sister's heavy footsteps crossed the room. I heard her say a muffled *hello,* a *hold on,* and then the whole house heard as she shouted my name.

I rolled off the cot and went upstairs. The phone was sitting on the counter. I stretched the cord into the living room and said, "Hello."

"Bet you didn't think it would be me," Karla said.

I smiled at that. "You'd be right. I figured I'd never hear from you again."

"You wish. So how's life in the frozen north?"

"Pretty much the way you left it," I said, then, a little softer, "Thanks for the car."

She chuckled. "You thank me now. Wait till you have to get that thing repaired. And remember, it pulls wicked to the right."

"I'll be careful," I said, then I asked the question I assumed she wanted to answer. "What's the weather like?"

"Nice. Not too hot. It was only like sixty today. But better than there."

"It is. And you got no snow."

"You should come down. You'd like it. Lot of cool people."

I was tempted to say, "Like Scott?" but I let it go. Instead I said, "Thanks, but I don't think I could afford it."

"That's just an excuse and you know it. Come on, you were all, 'I gotta change.' What happened to that?"

"I'm working on it," I said, and before she could ask for proof, I asked, "You get a job yet?"

"First day. The Del Mar Hotel, right on the beach. Minimum wage, but they bump you up quick. They're hiring like crazy. Scott's brother has connections. He can find you something."

Everybody offering me a job.

"You can stay with us. We got the space, as long as you don't mind sharing the bathroom."

"Hmmm. Fun."

"Oh, stop. It's not bad. And there's a lot of girls down here, too. They're so hot, *I* even notice them."

"Maybe. We'll see."

"You're an ass," she said, and I could hear that smile in her voice that I missed. "You want *real* change? Come and get it. You're not going to find it up there."

"I think I'll stick around here for a while."

"Why? There's nothing there to—Wait a minute." She stopped and the phone got quiet. "What's her name?"

I laughed. "I don't know what you mean."

"Nick. You can't lie to me. Who is she?"

"Her name's Dawn. You don't know her. And we're not dating or anything. We're hanging out is all."

"You banging her?"

"*What?* No."

"Bullshit. I don't believe it."

"Believe whatever you want," I said. "But it's true."

"You like her?"

I had to think about that one. I knew the situation, knew what my chances were, and I could see where it would all end up going, which was nowhere. But I also knew how I felt. "Yeah, she's all right."

"She feel the same way?"

"I don't know yet."

"You want some advice?"

"No."

"You got to be a good listener."

"Thank you, Princess Obvious."

She sighed, and for a moment it felt as if she was sitting right next to me, and not way the hell down in Florida. "I know you, Nick. You focus on the stuff you want to hear and miss everything else."

"I hear you."

"I know you do," she said. "But are you listening?"

FRIDAY, DECEMBER 30

GEORGE LOOKED AT HIS LIST.

"It's New Year's Eve weekend, so we're gonna need a lot of ice. Bag up what's in the machine. Fifty bags, not one bag less, then—"

"Sorry, can't do it," I said.

George's eyes popped and he made this choking sound. "*What?*"

"I said I can't do it." I pointed at the ice maker. It was twice the size of a refrigerator, and it had a metal door that swung open to the bin where the ice was stored. "The machine shuts off at four hundred pounds. Says so right there on the sign. The bags hold ten pounds. There's not enough for fifty bags."

"That's plenty," he said, his face starting to glow red. "Just bag it up."

"I'll bag as many as I can," I said. "But it won't be fifty."

He inched closer to me and did his best to stare me down—nostrils flaring, mouth all bunched up. He held on for a good ten seconds before looking away. "Fine. Just get it done."

I smiled, but he missed it, busy scribbling something on

his clipboard. "And when you finish *that,* clean the bathroom. It's disgusting. And it better be *really* clean, or you'll be doing it again."

There was more, but I tuned him out, enjoying how good it felt to stand up for something as small as a bag of ice.

I WAS AT the register when Jay walked in.

The last time I'd seen him was the night me and Karla had ended up at the college party. That was also the night—apparently—that Jay and the others had all decided that they'd be happier without some asshole named Nick hanging around. I couldn't speak for them, but as far as I was concerned, this new arrangement was turning out all right.

I'd worked every Friday night for the past six months—Jay *had* to know I'd be there. So that meant he wanted something. I smiled. No need to be a jerk about it. It wasn't his fault that my life needed a major overhaul. If anything, I owed him for helping motivate me to change, just by being himself.

"What's up?"

Jay came straight to the counter. "I wanna get some beer for tomorrow. You gonna be cool?"

I nodded. "Better get it tonight, though. Georgie says he's working the register tomorrow. No ID, no beer."

"All right," Jay said. "But I wanna get a half keg. Doable?"

"No, man. Sorry. Just go with cases. With a keg there's a deposit and you gotta rent the tap . . ."

"You got a half keg of Bud back there?"

"Yeah, but . . ."

"Okay, I'll take that."

"Dude, you're not listening," I said. "You gotta have a credit card to get the tap."

"Just let me borrow one. I'll bring it back Sunday."

I rubbed a hand across my face. "Look, get a bunch of cases. It's easier and there's no—"

"Why you gotta be an asshole?"

I stopped. "*What?*"

"It's not like I'm gonna steal it, you wuss."

"I didn't say that. I only said that with a keg—"

"Forget it," Jay said, hands up all dramatic, backing toward the door. "They told me you'd be a dick about it."

"Jay, you can *get as much beer*—"

"Your problem is that you're a little bitch," Jay said. Then his head snapped back and his feet flew up and he was out the door, coming down hard on the pavement by his car. Zod followed him, kicking him once in the balls, then again in the back, bending over to clock him on the ear. Jay had his hands up around his face now, but Zod was done, stepping around him, onto the sidewalk, and into the store.

"Hey, look at you," Zod said, dusting his hands as he walked. "Nametag and everything. How's it going?"

"It goes," I said, looking past Zod, watching as Jay stumbled himself into the driver's seat of his car.

"Not too busy?"

"No, not really."

Zod followed my gaze to the parking lot as the car raced away. "You get a lot of assholes in here?"

I looked right at him. "A few."

"Well, it comes with the job."

"Yeah," I said. "I suppose."

Zod tossed a twenty on the counter. "Give me a couple packs of Zig-Zags."

I reached behind for the rolling papers. That's when I noticed George, peeking around the coffee machine, keeping a safe distance from the register. I rang up the sale and gave Zod his change, counting it back like I'd been taught to do.

Zod stuffed the bills in his pocket, leaving the coins on the counter. "You still thinking over Reg's offer?"

Dawn had been right—they didn't hear me. Or they didn't listen. I shook my head. "I'm not working for him."

"Think of it as working for the higher-highers. Reg's bosses."

"I'm not working for any of them."

"Not yet. But you'll get sick of this bullshit job," Zod said, then, raising his voice and pointing straight at George, "and working for some douchebag."

I didn't turn, but I watched Zod's eyes as they tracked George scurrying to the back room.

"So, anyway," Zod said, pulling a fat baggie of weed out of his coat pocket as he shuffled to the door. "You know where to find us."

IT WAS OBVIOUS that George had run out of jobs for me to do when he told me to straighten out the comic book stand. But I did it. Nothing else to do but wait for the minute hand to crawl up the last twenty minutes to midnight.

That's when Dawn came in.

George was at the register, and even if he had recognized her as the girl who had burned him for ten bucks, he wouldn't have said anything. He just smiled and did that half-nod thing, leaning forward as she passed, watching her ass as she went down the aisle.

"Excuse me, sir," she said as she walked toward me. "Do you have the latest issue of *Playgirl*?"

I held out a comic book. "No, ma'am. But I do have *The Avengers*."

She waved it off. "I'm more of a *Catwoman* fan myself." She stretched on her toes and pulled a copy of *Cosmo* off the top rack, reading the cover aloud. "'Are You Romantic? Take the Quiz!' Ha. I'd fail."

"I doubt that," I said, no idea why.

"'Sexy by Spring! Exercise Your Way to Excitement!' They lost me at exercise."

"Funny, they had me at sexy."

She tapped the cover. "Here's one I need to read. 'Escape from Relationships with Sickos.'" She flipped to the table of contents, then flipped to the middle of the magazine and ran her eyes over the first page of the article. "Damn. I *do* need to read this."

Back at the register, George coughed loudly. I ignored him. "What brings you way out here on a Friday night?"

"You," Dawn said, poking me in the chest with the edge of the magazine. "What are you doing after work?"

Going home and going to bed. That's what the plan was, but that's not what you say to a hot girl poking you in the chest with a *Cosmo.* So I said, "Haven't decided yet. What do you suggest?"

She smiled. "I'll swing by at midnight," she said, then turned, walked down the aisle and out of the store.

I watched her go. So did George, clearly not noticing the magazine in her hand.

AT MIDNIGHT GEORGE locked the front door, mumbled a *good night,* got in his car, and drove off.

There was no sign of her, so I sat in my car, engine running, heat on high, waiting. Two songs on the radio later, a blue and white Beetle pulled in next to me. She rolled down her window and said, "Follow me." I did — out of the parking lot, south toward the mall, then right on Ridge Road, past the shopping plaza, the Kmart, and the movie theater, past a dozen car dealerships, past the diner, past any place I could imagine her taking me. Ahead on the right was a Chinese take-out restaurant. She slowed and hit her left directional, pulling into the parking lot of the Wishing Well Motel, the orange neon sign flashing NO VACANCY.

Everybody knew about the Wishing Well. It was the no-tell motel guys joked about when they hit on the girls at school, the post-prom destination no one ever got to. The building was long and low and drab — twenty rooms, no pool, no cable, no pets. Its only selling point was the tall row of thick hedges that hid the narrow parking lot from the street. For all their macho bragging, no one I hung out with had ever been this close.

I parked next to Dawn's car and got out.

"I know it's a dump," Dawn said. "But I just had to have a night away."

I thought of the army cot in the basement that was waiting for me at home. "I can relate."

We walked to the room. The curtains were closed, but there was a light on inside. Dawn put the key in the door and paused. "Close your eyes."

"Why?"

"Because I want it to be a surprise."

Like Reg waiting with a baseball bat? No, thanks. "Just go," I said. "It's cold out here."

"Ugh, you're no fun," she said, and then she opened the door.

It was a surprise.

The first thing I saw were the balloons. On the floor, on the bed, some spilling outside. Then I saw the silver streamers hanging from the ceiling, shimmering in the draft. On the nightstand there was an ice bucket with a bottle of champagne and two paper cups. And taped on the wall above the TV, a handmade sign. HAPPY NEW YEAR!

I stepped inside and looked around. Dawn shut the door, threw the bolt, and put the chain on.

I said, "What's this for?"

"Duh. What do you *think* it's for?"

"But New Year's Eve is tomorrow."

"I *know* that," she said. "I'll be spending it with Sir Reginald and his pals. Imagine how much fun *that'll* be." She took off her coat, hanging it on the hook by the door, then she sat on the edge of the bed to unzip her knee-high boots. "I wanted to start the New Year off right, and that meant I couldn't start it with them. So I'm starting it with you."

I wanted to tell her that was the nicest thing anybody

had said to me in a long, long time, but it sounded lame in my head, so instead I said, "I'll open the champagne."

"Wait, not yet." She scooted up the bed, moving the pillows out of her way to sit with her back against the headboard. She took a travel alarm clock out of her purse and set the time back to 11:58. "According to *my* clock, we've got two minutes."

"It'll take me that long to figure out how to open it."

"Sit up here with me, then. We'll watch the second hand go round."

I kicked off my sneakers and sat down next to her, close, but not too close, the bed creaking under us. Dawn laughed. "Geez, I bet this thing makes some noise."

"I'll try not to breathe." I put a pillow on my lap and set the alarm clock on top. It was a poor table but a good cover.

She leaned over and took something out of her purse. "Here, put this on."

I held it up. "For real?"

"I insist."

I shrugged and put the glittery green party hat on my head, pulling the thin elastic band under my chin. "How's it look?"

Dawn adjusted her hair around a cardboard HAPPY 1978! tiara. "About as stupid as this. Let's get that bottle open."

It took longer than I thought, and when the plastic

cork popped, champagne sprayed the bedspread, new spots blending in with the old.

"Here's to new beginnings," Dawn said, tapping her cup against mine.

It was cheap champagne — the $4.99 sticker was still on the bottle — but I knew that if I lived to be one hundred, no drink would ever taste as good.

"Soooo," Dawn said, running a finger around the top of the paper cup. "You know what I want to do now?"

I had ideas — lots of them — but I said, "No clue."

"I wanna get under the covers with you, then cuddle up close . . ." She paused and looked up into my eyes. "And watch monster movies all night long."

I smiled anyway. "Sounds good to me."

"Honest?"

"Honest."

"You're not going to try anything, are you?"

"Scout's honor," I said, holding up my hand. "We'll just watch movies. This is *your* New Year's."

She looked at me and her eyes got soft, and she said, "You know, that's the nicest thing anybody's said to me in a long, long time."

THE GLOW-IN-THE-DARK HANDS of the travel alarm clock read 3:15.

Dawn's head was on my shoulder, one arm under her

pillow, the other across my chest, her breathing soft and easy. I left the TV on, volume low, and thought about what had happened.

Technically *nothing* had happened. We got under the covers. She cuddled next to me. We drank champagne and watched monster movies. No sex, no making out, no roaming hands. She still had on her black Cheap Trick T-shirt and bright red underwear. I still had on the white shirt and tie I wore to work and my boxers. If she had noticed the hourlong, tent-pole bulge—and there was no way to miss it—she had acted like it wasn't there. I didn't know if I should feel relieved or disappointed. But I did know that I was happy. It was a different kind of happy—and maybe that wasn't even the right word—but as I watched Godzilla lumber through downtown Tokyo and felt Dawn's warm breath on my arm, *happy* pretty much summed it up. And when she whispered, the words seemed to float by.

"It's New Year's in Vietnam."

It was strange and I had to think it through, trying to remember which way the world turned. "Not yet," I said, softening my voice to match hers. "They still got a half a day to go."

"They have a different New Year's. The traditional one, anyway. They call it *Tet Nguyen Dan.* It means the feast of the first morning of the first day."

"Nice."

"Yeah." She paused, took a shaky breath. "Nine years ago today, on the first morning of the first day of Tet, a hand grenade landed next to my father."

I heard myself gasp. She pressed her hand to my chest.

"It's okay," she said. "It was a long time ago. I was pretty young. My sister was only three. She never really knew him, not even in her way. I suppose I didn't either. It was different for my mother. She's still all messed up. Probably why she can't keep a job. It's the worst around the holidays. She started early this year, a month before Thanksgiving. All of a sudden, we had no money. Nothing. We were going to lose the apartment." She paused, sighed. "That's when I took the job with Reg."

"Damn."

She laughed. "More like damned."

"Can't you get anything from the army? They must have benefits or something for families."

"It was the marines, and, yes, there's benefits. But only for families. My parents never bothered to get married. Way too traditional for *my* mother," she said, her tone hinting at what she thought of the idea. "So we're not considered family."

"What about your grandparents?"

"Never met my mother's parents. From the little she's said about them, that's a good thing. My father's parents blame my mother for their son getting killed. Funny thing, she wanted him to run to Canada. Anyway, nothing from Gram and Gramps. I suppose we could go to court, prove that he was the father, but that would take money. And if we won, his parents could turn around and sue for custody of my sister. They'd win, too. My mother can barely take care of herself. She doesn't want to get better, either. My sister and I should be on our own. It's pretty much all on me right now." She straightened her legs and stretched, then cuddled closer, putting her head on my chest. Two minutes later, she was asleep.

And right then, at that dead-quiet moment in that no-tell motel on a make-believe New Year's Eve and a god-awful anniversary, I knew I was the biggest loser on the planet.

Oh, poor Nicky, you have to live in basement of your parents' house.

Your mommy and daddy don't love each other anymore.

You don't have any friends.

Boo-hoo-hoo.

But what made it worse, next to me in bed—was she always that tiny?—lay somebody a lot braver and stronger than me.

And I knew I would do anything for her.

I WOKE TO the sound of water running.

One eye opened.

A saggy, green velvet curtain with sunlight bleeding in

around the edges, an empty champagne bottle on the floor, one of my sneakers, a toothbrush rapping against the sink in the bathroom.

It took me a few minutes, but I pieced it together.

I'd slept with a few girls, but I'd never woken up next to one, and I wasn't sure what came next. Did I offer to take her to breakfast? Go get her a coffee? And the things she told me, was it safe to bring any of it up, or was I supposed to pretend I'd been too sleepy to remember? I was still thinking it through when I heard the water turn off. Too late to do anything but lay there.

"Rise and shine," Dawn said as she came out of the bathroom. Her hair was a mess and her eyes looked different without makeup, somehow larger and not as dark. I thought it was a good look. She dropped her toothbrush into her purse and sat crossed-legged on the bed.

I propped a pillow behind my head. "What time do we gotta be out of here?"

"You in a rush?"

"I don't want it to cost you any more than it has."

She laughed. "What, you think they rent by the hour or something? Trust me, the room was worth the whole twenty-four dollars it cost. Oh, and thanks again for not trying anything."

"No problem. Well, maybe *some* problem . . ."

She smiled. "You have no idea how long I've wanted to

just lounge around like that. Nobody having to snort lines or spark a bowl first. Like I'm so awful they've got to be stoned to sit next to me."

"It was fun," I said. I meant it, too. "Definitely a first. For me, anyway."

"Me too," she said. "Believe it or not, that was one of my new year's resolutions from *last* year."

"To watch monster movies in a crappy motel room?"

"No," she said, looking into my eyes. "To spend a wonderful night with a great guy."

I felt my face flush, and I wanted to laugh, but I could tell Dawn wasn't kidding this time. I took a deep breath, savoring the moment. "Glad I could make one of your wishes come true."

Dawn smiled at that, a different type of smile, her eyes narrowing as she reached down for the bottom of her T-shirt, pulling it off and tossing it to the floor in one graceful move. "Now it's my turn," she said.

1978

MONDAY, JANUARY 2

THE NEW YEAR WAS ONLY TWO DAYS OLD, BUT I WAS CERTAIN that 1978 was going to be the best year of my life.

This was the fresh start I'd been looking for. Well, a start of a start anyway. The whole reinventing-myself thing was taking a lot longer than I thought it would. I'd been at it almost a month and I was still living in my parents' basement, I still had the same crappy job, and I still had no real idea what to do next. Kind of hard to find a new life when you're living in the old one. The only thing that seemed to be going according to plan was my wardrobe change. I had four different ties now, and a few more button-down shirts, and I liked the way they made me stand out from the crowd. Yet almost every morning, I pulled out one of my old concert T-shirts before remembering that I didn't wear those anymore. I kept my list in my wallet and I was going to stick to it—that was one of the things on it—but there were moments when I'd wonder if a four-line, eight-word list was going to be enough. But it was something—and it was as close to a fresh start as I was going to get.

And it started with Dawn.

That morning in the motel room? The single greatest morning of my life.

The motel manager had to call the room twice—once to remind Dawn that checkout was at ten a.m., a second time, close to noon, to tell us to get the hell out. I hadn't seen Dawn since, but I knew it would be like that, meeting up when we could, where we could. For now, anyway.

"I wasn't kidding about my new year's resolutions. I want a new life," she had said as we showered, slipping her arms around my soapy neck. "I just gotta figure out how to get it."

The sound of ice scraping off the windshield brought me back to the moment. I flexed my fingers to keep them warm. It was cold and dark and quiet, the fresh foot of snow deadening any sound in the neighborhood. I could barely hear my car as it idled. It was weird, even a little scary, but it was better than listening to my sister yelling as she got the girls ready for school, better than hearing my father making up stories as to why he'd be home late again, better than hearing my mother's not-so-subtle hints that I move out already.

It was too early to go to school, but I figured I'd stop at the donut place on the way in, kill some time there as I skimmed the book I was supposed to have read over break. Or maybe not. Maybe I'd simply sit there and think about the weekend some more. It was nice to have options.

I backed out of the driveway and headed down the road.

That's when I saw the blue and white VW parked at the corner.

Her car was running and Dawn sat behind the steering wheel. I pulled up alongside, and she looked over at me. Even through the fogged-up window, I could tell something was wrong. I motioned for her to follow me, then I drove to the mall, parking in an area that had already been plowed. She parked next to me and unlocked the passenger door. I got out of my car and into hers, and was expecting to see a black eye or a swollen lip, but she looked all right, no makeup covering a bruise. She took my hand, squeezed it. I could feel her leg shaking.

"Sorry," she said. "I don't mean to freak you out or anything, I just had to see you, that's all."

"What's up?"

Dawn looked away and made a sound like a laugh. She drummed her fingers on the steering wheel, shook her head. "You're not going to believe me."

"Try me."

"Okay. Listen. I think . . ." She sighed, took a deep breath, and said, "I think they did something to Freddie."

I could see the guy—short, a bit dumpy, hint of a mustache, his head snapping back when Reg slapped him for talking out of turn. "Who are *they?*"

"Who else," Dawn said. "Reg, Cory, Steve, Lester. All of them."

"Why?"

She shook her head. "Something to do with missing drugs. Or money. It doesn't matter. Something went missing, and they think he took it."

"Did he?"

"How am I supposed to know? I don't talk to any of them if I can help it. Especially Freddie. I told you, I don't trust him."

I could guess how it went down. Freddie saw how much there was — coke or cash — and figured either Reg wouldn't notice or wouldn't care if a little was missing. Only Reg *would* notice, and he *would* care, and he'd know who to blame. "What do you think they did to him?"

Dawn closed her eyes. After a long pause, she said, "I think they killed him."

"*What?*"

"See? I knew you wouldn't believe me."

"I didn't say that. I'm just . . . I don't know . . . it seems kinda —"

"Psycho?"

"Yeah, but —"

She pulled her hand away. "Forget I said anything. Just go."

"Geez, calm down. I believe you. I'm just not used to stuff like that."

"And I am?"

"Okay, okay," I said. "Cool it for a second. We gotta think here."

"Think about what?"

"What we're gonna do."

"What do you mean, 'What *we're* gonna do'? You're not part of this."

"No," I said. "But you are."

Her eyes started to water. "Don't be stupid."

"It comes naturally."

"Why do you care what happens to me?"

I knew why. But now wasn't the time. "I don't know," I said. "I just do."

She looked away.

Across the parking lot, a pair of plows cleared the spaces near the Sears, ramming the snow into piles as tall as the lamp poles. It was warm inside the car. I unzipped my coat and watched the plows for a while, then I said, "We have to go to the police."

Dawn kept her head turned. "You're crazy."

"If you tell them what you know—"

"I don't *know* anything. I only know what I think I might know."

"That makes no sense."

She chuckled. "Tell me about it."

"But they'd have to investigate."

"And what do you think they're going to find? Freddie's body in the basement? Reg is insane, but he's not stupid. If they killed Freddie, *nobody's* gonna find him. Ever."

"Fine," I said. "Then you gotta get out of there."

"Why? I didn't take anything. I'm not *that* crazy."

No, I thought, *but us being together with Reg in the picture, now that's crazy.* I kept that thought to myself and said, "I just think it'd be safer if you went somewhere else."

She turned. "And go where, Nick? Really. Where should I go? You tell me."

"Venice."

"Italy?"

"Florida. I have a friend who lives there. Her name's Karla. She'd be cool with it, and you could—"

"No, I couldn't, Nick," she said. "My sister needs me. I could never leave her. My mother, well . . ."

"Take your sister with you. You could crash at Karla's place a few weeks. She'll help you get a job, find a place to live. Trust me, she wouldn't mind at all," I said, wondering if any of it was true.

Dawn leaned back in her seat. I watched as she played it out in her head, her eyes open, her lower lip curled in between her teeth.

"You could leave today," I added.

"Yeah, right," she said. I heard her mumble to herself and laugh, then she mumbled something else, and the laugh was gone. After a long, quiet minute, she looked over. "Would you go with me?"

Whoa.

I wasn't expecting that.

Asking me for money, a ride to the bus station, sure, but asking me to run off? What was she thinking? I hardly knew her. Yeah, the sex was amazing, but what about my life here? My family, my education, my future? She wanted me to give it all up, just like that, start with nothing—*less* than nothing—in another city, another state. Yeah, I know, I said I wanted a change, but was I really ready to make that big of a leap? And when we got there—*if* we made it that far—the only thing we'd have would be each other, and who knew how long that would last. Plus we'd have her sister to take care of. What if she needed more care than we could give her? And if Dawn was right, if Reg did kill Freddie, he wouldn't let her go. If she took off, he'd try to track her down. He wasn't as big as he thought he was, but he could still have contacts, the higher-highers Zod hinted at. Dawn had no one, so she clung to me, hoping to be rescued. But if it went bad—and why wouldn't it?—I'd get pulled down with her.

We didn't stand a chance.

I was about to tell her all that.

Then I looked in her eyes.

"Yeah. I'll go with you."

THE WAITRESS REFILLED our cups, putting the check facedown on the table. The morning rush was over, so we could take our time. I covered the last pancake with blueberry syrup. "Pancakes are why they invented mornings."

Dawn reached behind and grabbed the small basket of creamers and sugar packets from the next booth. She stacked four sugar packets together, tapping them on the table like a deck of cards before ripping off the tops and pouring it all into her cup. "I'm warning you now, I make a wicked omelet. Ham, cheese, tomatoes, onions, a little crumbled bacon. I'll make you forget all about your pancakes."

I didn't doubt it. She'd already made me forget about a lot of things.

"When we get to Florida, I'll get a job as a short-order cook at some breakfast place like this. I'd probably have to start as a waitress, but once they see me behind the grill, they'll promote me. That's what I'd do. I mean, not forever — I want my own restaurant someday — but just to start. What about you? What's your dream job?"

She wasn't the first person to ask me that question.

It seemed to come up at least once a year, starting back in kindergarten. Back then, me and every other kid in America were going to be astronauts. I could do a really good drawing of me in a silver spacesuit, floating around a Mercury space capsule, a sure sign that I had the right stuff for the job. By sixth grade it began to feel like school was never going to end, so I didn't think much about what I'd do if it did. Then eighth grade came and that summer I saw Zod stab a guy. That led to me spending time on the job with some adults who didn't treat me like a dumb kid, who told me I was brave and honest and tough for testifying in court. It was only a few weeks of my life, but it stuck with me, gave me something bigger to think about. So I told her.

"I'd be a cop."

She sipped her coffee and looked at me over the top of her mug. "I can see it."

"Is that a good thing?"

"It could be. Some of the cops I know are cool. They'll bust you if you're breaking the law — well, *most* laws — but they're not like assholes or anything. You can trust them, know what I mean? They're not on some power trip. They take care of people. You'd be like that."

I shrugged, afraid to admit that I liked the way it sounded.

Dawn flipped over the check. "Damn. I should've stuck with toast." She pulled her wallet from her purse and put a ten on the table. "We won't be able to eat like this when we're on the road."

"What do you think we'll need, cash-wise?"

"The Beetle's too small for three people—"

"Three?"

"Terri," Dawn said, like it was obvious. "My sister. That's why we'd have to take your car. Is that okay?"

"It should be," I said, not sure if it would be.

"Pintos are good on gas, but it's a long way and we're assuming we won't have any car troubles. And once we get there, we can't be sponging off your friend."

"Karla won't mind."

"But *I* will," Dawn said. "I don't want to be owing someone right off the bat. That's how I screwed up last time."

There was a story behind that line, I was sure of it, but I didn't want to hear it. The less I knew about her time with Reg, the better.

"We don't need much," Dawn said. "I think with two thousand, we'll be okay."

"Two *thousand?*"

"I know, it sounds like a lot—"

"Because it *is*."

"Not when you consider we're moving all the way to Florida."

"We'll get jobs when we get there. That'll give us some cash."

"Right, but even if we get hired the first day, it's going to be a couple weeks before we'd get paid. And Terri's going to need stuff right away." She opened her wallet again and ran a thumb over the bills, counting as she went. "I've got eighty-five dollars to my name."

I didn't need to check my wallet. "I got thirty-two bucks on me. Friday I'll get a check for sixty-three fifty-two. My regular pay plus holiday pay. Then next Friday another one for the same amount."

"Okay," Dawn said, writing the numbers on a napkin. "That works out to . . ."

"Two hundred forty-four dollars and four cents."

Dawn smiled. "So that means we're still—"

"One thousand seven hundred fifty-five dollars and ninety-six cents short."

"Now you're just showing off."

"No. If I was showing off, I'd tell you that at two sixty-five an hour and my current work schedule, it's going to take me . . ." I closed my eyes, rounded up and did the math. "Fifty-six weeks to earn the rest. Not counting taxes or spending money. At that rate, we're still here this time next year."

Dawn slumped against the back of the booth. "I knew it was too good to be true."

"We can still go," I said. "We'll figure something out along the way."

"Come on, Nick. Be realistic."

"Well, we gotta do something. It's a new year. It's the best time to make a change. Plus it's warm in Florida."

"I can look for a job again," Dawn said. "Reg went ballistic last time I tried. He thinks it's insulting if his *girlfriend* has to work."

"But it's okay to hit her."

"Exactly."

"I'll see if I can get more hours at the Stop-N-Go. Not that it'll help much."

Dawn's eyes went wide and she leaned forward, dropping her voice to a whisper. "There's tons of cash at Reg's place. I could just, you know, slip a few bucks off the pile now and then, miscount the money . . ."

I laughed. "Are you insane? You want to end up like Freddie?"

"Geez, hold it down." She glanced around the restaurant, the closest customers five booths away and the waitresses all huddled by the register. "Reg is coked-out all the time. The guys all know he's losing it. He's so paranoid about them, he wouldn't suspect it was me. And, besides, Freddie was sloppy. I'm not."

"I bet that's what he thought, too. So don't even think about it."

She smiled.

"Hey," I said. "I'm serious. You gotta promise me you won't do anything like that."

"Fine," she said, crossing her heart. "I promise."

I sipped my coffee. I had already run down a dozen moneymaking ideas in my head. The ones that made sense—getting a second job, selling my stereo and records—made little money or took too long, and the ones that were crazy—faking a holdup at the Stop-N-Go, buying a whole roll of scratch-off lottery tickets—were just really stupid.

That left one idea.

It made sense, sort of, and it wasn't too crazy.

There was some risk, sure, almost enough to take it off the list.

Almost.

I thought it through again, and it was starting to sound all right.

"Reg's guys," I said. "How's he keep them around?"

"What do you think? He pays them."

"A lot?"

She looked up. "You want to *work* for him?"

"Why not?"

"It's dangerous."

"I know that," I said. "I'll be careful."

"*He's* dangerous. He's got a short fuse. You piss him off . . ."

I remembered how Reg clocked Freddie for daring to speak, and I remembered the dark look in Reg's eyes when he thought Dawn was being sarcastic. But I also remembered that I had weathered Reg's stare, that I stood there, nose to coke-dusted nose, and didn't blink, all but challenging Reg to try to steal from the Stop-N-Go.

It was true, Reg was dangerous.

But he was also a businessman.

A businessman who needed someone he could trust, someone who wouldn't just tell him what he wanted to hear, someone who gave his word and stuck by it.

Someone like me.

I looked down at my hands and caught my reflection in the coffee, staring back up at me. I flicked my wrist and the image swirled away.

"Tell me about Freddie's job," I said.

I KNOCKED TWICE on the door and waited.

I could hear the TV but no voices. Dawn had told me that there was always someone there, but that didn't mean that they would open the door, especially if they didn't recognize the vehicle. I'd been there twice before, once parking right out front in my own car, but who could say what they would or would not remember. Reg might have already forgotten the offer.

Dawn had spent fifteen minutes trying to talk me out of taking the job, then another twenty telling me how to play it. "Don't act all cool," she had said. "You'll only look nervous. Just be yourself. And if you change your mind—"

"I'm not going to change my mind."

"If you do, do it before the run starts. Because once it starts, there's no stopping it."

I rapped the door again, harder this time, but the laugh track on *The Brady Bunch* still sounded louder. Zod's red Camaro was in the driveway, and there was a Toyota pickup parked on the side lawn. There were tire tracks in the snow that led to a garage out back. I assumed that was where Reg parked whatever it was he drove. Probably a T-bird. Reg looked the type.

I knocked a third time—loud and long enough not to be ignored.

It was funny, I knew I should be scared, but I wasn't. There was no question that Reg was crazy dangerous, maybe a killer, and working for him—even for a day—could get me in shit so deep I'd never see daylight. The smart thing would have been to forget the whole idea—the job, Florida, a new life. Everything. My old life was survivable. Boring, but survivable. It would be stupid to throw it away now just for the chance to play warlord and come to the rescue of some black-haired princess. But as the deadbolts clicked back, it didn't feel stupid at all.

"Well, well, well," Cory said, letting me in, then locking the door behind me. "Look who came to visit."

I stomped the snow off my boots and unzipped my jacket. The TV played to an empty room, and there was no one at the table. And instead of pot or beer, the room smelled of pasta sauce.

"Fun day at school?"

I hadn't gone, but I didn't want any questions, so I said, "It was school."

"You reconsidering Reg's offer?"

I shrugged. "Maybe."

"Don't play games. Either you want in or not. Don't waste our time."

"Yeah, I want in," I said, the words sounding strange as I said them. "Just a job, that's all. Nothing more than that."

Cory laughed. "No shit, dude. Sit down. I'll get the man."

I sat on the couch and had a look around.

There was an end table next to the couch and, on it, a lamp, an ashtray, and a chewed-off pizza crust. On the floor was a dirty carpet, a beer can, a *Penthouse* magazine, and a lot of cigarette burns. On the TV, Marcia Brady was about to get her nose broken by a football. At the other end of the room were the table and chairs where Reg held court, his dumpy castle in a dumpy part of town. Crime paid, but apparently not enough for decorating.

Down the hall I could hear mumbled voices, then a door opening, and then there was Reg, strutting into the room. He took a seat at the table and fished a cigarette out of the pack in his shirt pocket. There was a lighter on the table, and he used it, sucking in a long drag, letting it out slow. The gray-white smoke hung in the air between us. "What do you want?"

I swallowed. "You said I could do some jobs for you."

Reg slung a skinny arm over the back of his chair and took another drag. "You said no."

"I uh . . . I changed my mind."

More smoke. "Maybe I did too."

I didn't know what to say to that, so I sat there and waited. Half a cigarette later, Reg said, "Steve tells me I can trust you. But I don't trust anybody. Not even him. What makes you so damn special?"

I shrugged. "I don't know."

"He banging your sister or something?"

It wasn't meant as a joke, but I had to laugh.

Reg almost smiled. "You never know with that bastard." He ground out his cigarette on a paper plate. "Why do you want to work for me?"

"I need the money."

"Don't we all."

"I have a job at the Stop-N-Go, but it doesn't pay much."

"You told me all about it last time. Or did you forget?"

"No, I didn't think you'd, um, that . . ."

"You didn't think I'd remember," Reg said. "Let me tell you something, Nick, I don't forget anything."

I felt my stomach dip.

"You know why I can trust you, Nick?"

"Because Steve said . . ."

"I don't need Steve's help, you got that?" He lit another cigarette and threw the lighter down on the table. It bounced once, then fell to the floor. "I know I can trust you, Nick, because you're not stupid. Stupid people do stupid things. Like talk to cops. Now, smart people—people like *you*—they know better. They know the business they're in and know that it comes with risks. Don't do the crime if you can't do the time. You follow me, Nick?"

"Yeah."

"Good to know. 'Cause if you're not . . ." Reg shook his head.

"No, I got it."

Reg took a drag on his cigarette, held it in as he thought. "Stupid people. You'd be surprised how many there are. They rip me off—I come for them and get what's mine. And when I find them, that's when things get ugly. Baseball bat to the jaw, hammer on some knuckles. Steve likes that shit. He stuck a knife clean through a guy's arm once, if you can believe it."

I could believe it. I saw it happen.

"Nothing personal. Just business," Reg said. "Stupid people, they don't get that. Smart people understand. That's why I like doing business with smart people. People like you."

My chest was pounding and my throat was too dry to swallow, yet I kept my eyes up, kept my legs from shaking. A voice in the back of my head was yelling something, but the words Dawn had whispered that New Year's Eve morning drowned it all out.

Reg twirled his cigarette between his long, bony fingers. "So, Nick, let's do business."

It was close to ten p.m., and I was driving down a road I'd never been on when I saw the flashing red lights in the rearview mirror.

Technically, I shouldn't be driving after nine, but once the cops found the cocaine on the floor of the back seat, they probably wouldn't even mention the time.

The plan had sounded smooth when Reg had explained it.

"You know the McDonald's on Lyell Ave.? Be there eight thirty on the dot. Park in the back, driver's side close to the chainlink fence, but not too close. Leave the door unlocked. Go in and buy some something. *I don't care, buy anything.* When you come out, your car will be locked and there'll be a gym bag on the floor. Leave it there. Then head west on Ridge Road. This is the address. It's way the hell in Lockport, so you better have enough gas. *No shit you don't know where it is.* There's a map on the back. It starts at the Exxon station right when you get into town. When you get there, go to the side door and knock. They'll do the rest."

So at eight thirty—after a quick stop at an office supply store—I parked at the McDonald's, went in, bought some fries, came out to find the car locked and a gym bag on the floor of the back seat. I left it there and headed west, stopping ninety minutes later at the Exxon station to check the map, then holding the map in one hand as I drove, trying to match pencil lines and misspelled street names to the real thing. I rolled up to a dark intersection, looked both ways, and went straight.

That's when I saw the flashing lights.

Instinctively, I checked the speedometer—thirty in a thirty-five. Not speeding.

No. *They knew.*

I could hit the gas and take off like in the movies, maybe get a whole mile down the road before the cops had me.

I could wait till the cop came to the window, and then punch it, but that would just piss off the cop and probably get me shot.

I flipped up the directional and pulled to the side of the road, my heart ripping apart, my nuts crawling into my gut.

I'd have to play it cool.

Is there a problem, officer? Oh, I thought I came to a complete stop. No, it won't happen again. My license? Of course. I know it's after my driving curfew, but it's just that I'm kinda lost. What gym bag?

I could feel the sweat on my lip beading up, my left leg bouncing, my hands wet and shaking. Play it cool? Wasn't happening. The lights inched closer as time dragged the terror out.

Please.

It wasn't my idea.

I just wanted to help her.

The siren wailed, growing louder, the lights brighter now, blinding in the rearview mirror.

Gimme a break.

Just this time.

I promise . . .

I swear to god . . .

Please.

The ear-splitting siren rattled the windows, and I felt my stomach heave as red light filled the inside of the car before flying past, disappearing down the long, empty road, leaving the dark and quiet night behind.

TWO MINUTES LATER, I was still sitting there, not moving, barely breathing, my hands still on the wheel, the right directional still clicking.

That's when the laughing started. A grunted chuckle at first, then a stupid giggle, then an all-out bust-up, the tears rolling down my cheeks as I held my sides. It went on for longer than it was worth, but it felt good, and it helped uncramp my stomach and slow the leg shakes. I wiped the sweat from my hands, took a dozen deep breaths, then flicked the directional the other way, and pulled back onto the road. As for that voice in my head, the one making all the promises? I cranked up the Ramones and made it go away.

» » »

THE GUY WITH the beard and glasses said, "What are you, like, fifteen?"

I sat up, which was hard to do on the beanbag chair. "I'm twenty," I lied.

"Like hell. You ain't even seventeen yet."

I was, but I'd said twenty, so I had to stick to it.

"Reg know how old you are?"

"Drop it, Dale," the fat man at the table said without turning, his eyes glued on the half-empty glass of bleach as the woman tapped in a pinch of white powder. At first it settled on the top, then clumps of grains broke away and floated down into the clear liquid, a white trail blooming as they dropped, clouding the bleach.

"It sure ain't pure," the fat man said.

"Never is," the woman said. "I'd say this has been stepped on four times." She poked at some grains on the table with a long, red fingernail. "Looks like they cut it with baking soda."

"Or baby laxative." The fat man ran a razor blade over a mirror, forming up a short thin line before bending over and snorting it up his nose in one jerky motion. He put his head back, sniffing hard. "I guess it's good enough."

The woman chopped at an aspirin-size pile, the razor blade clicking as it hit the glass. She looked at me. "Want a line?"

I shook my head. "No, thanks."

She smiled, then held a nostril shut as she ran her nose over the coke, sucking it off the mirror.

"So, kid," the fat man said. "Reg tell you how much?"

"He said you'd know."

The fat man grinned. "I do." He looked at the woman and gave her a nod that I wasn't supposed to see or understand. But I saw it, and I had a good idea what it meant. And I was ready for it.

"Wait here, I'll get the money," the fat man said.

"I can get it for you," Dale said, springing up from the couch. "It's all counted out and everything."

"No, you stay here, keep the kid company. Do a line if you want." The fat man lumbered across the room and down a dark hallway.

Reg had told me it would be like this. "They don't keep the cash in the living room," he had said. "They got it in one of the bedrooms. So don't get all freaked out when they go to get it." Yet even though I knew what was happening, I couldn't stop thinking that the fat man was busy loading a shotgun. Especially since it was taking so long.

Dale was back on the couch, sneezing and rubbing the end of his nose, when the fat man returned with a brown paper bag in one hand. "Here you go, kid," he said, tossing me the package. It was thinner than a paperback, and lighter, the bag wrapped on both ends with red rubber bands.

I stood and walked over and set the bag on the table. Then I reached inside my coat and took out a large manila envelope and a black marker. I flicked open the envelope and put the package inside. I was about to lick the flap and seal the envelope when the fat man said, "What the hell is this?"

I lowered the envelope. "I seal the envelope, you sign the back across the flap, that way when I hand it to Reg, he knows I didn't take anything out."

Dale started to say something, but the fat man cut him off. "You thinking I shorted you? Is that it? You don't trust me?"

"I trust you," I said. "But Reg doesn't trust me. I seal the envelope. You sign it. This way he can tell if it's been opened. He wants to make sure that he's getting *exactly* what you put in." I raised the envelope again, taking my time as I prepared to lick the flap. Out of the corner of my eye I saw the woman frantically mouthing something.

"Whose idea is this?"

I shrugged. It was Dawn's idea. She assumed they'd try to take advantage of me, but they didn't need to know that. I stuck my tongue out and moved the envelope closer, waiting.

"Hold on a second," the fat man said. "Did you say this was for *Reg?*"

"Yeah. Reg," I said, letting it play out.

The fat man slapped himself on the forehead. "You hear that, Dale, this is *Reg's* runner."

"I told you when he got—"

"Shut up, Dale," the fat man said. "You hear that, Meg? It's *Reg's* runner."

"I heard you," the woman said.

The fat man smiled. "Sorry, kid. Thought you were someone else. Give me that money. That's, uh, for another guy. Reg's money's in the safe."

I handed the man the package, and a few minutes later he was back, dropping the same paper bag—thicker and heavier now—into the envelope, sealing it himself, and signing the flap in big, sloppy cursive.

"Glad we got that straightened out," the fat man said. "That could have been confusing."

I stuffed the envelope inside my coat and zipped it up. "Yeah. I'd sure hate to have Reg mad at me."

The fat man gave a nervous laugh. "You got that right."

TUESDAY, JANUARY 3

IT HAD BEEN THE LONGEST MONDAY OF MY LIFE. I SLEPT good, though, and it was noon before I rolled out of my cot and climbed the basement steps to the kitchen.

I didn't think anyone was home, but when I came out of the bathroom, I noticed my mother sitting in the corner of the kitchen, smoking a cigarette. There were two cups of coffee on the table, so that meant my sister was there too. I could hear her upstairs on the phone now, crying to somebody named Bret.

"About time you got up," my mother said.

I grunted a greeting, then opened the fridge to survey my options.

"What time did you get in last night?"

"I don't know. About one." I moved the gallon of milk to the side, hoping to spot a slice of pizza.

"It was two forty," she said. "I know because you woke us all up."

"I was trying to be quiet. I didn't expect a Barbie playhouse on the basement stairs."

"Well, you should have looked. You know your nieces like to play there."

I tried the freezer. Unknowns wrapped in aluminum foil, bags of frozen peas, a carton of Rocky Road ice cream, two empty ice trays, an open box of baking soda. I went with the ice cream.

My mother flicked the ash off her cigarette. "Why didn't you turn on the light?"

There was only a little ice cream left, so I grabbed a spoon, stood by the sink, and ate it out of the carton. Between mouthfuls I said, "I was trying to be considerate."

"If you *were* trying to be considerate, you'd come home at a decent hour."

Another mouthful. "Something came up."

"Oh, I'm sure it did. Just like something came up yesterday when you should have been at school? They called and left a message. It's a good thing I erased it before your father got home." She looked past me to the clock on the stove. "I assume they'll be calling again today. You better hope your father isn't here to answer it."

I knew what would happen if my father heard that I had skipped school.

Nothing.

The family had been through it all before with my sisters. Back then, they had tried everything—punishments, behavior contracts, threats, bribes, counseling—none of it making the slightest difference. Those were rough years, filled with a lot of yelling and slammed doors and cop cars in the driveway. In the end, my sisters did what they wanted anyway. Eileen kept sleeping with Allen until she got knocked up and married, and Gail kept doing whatever.

So far my parents had had it pretty easy with me. The key, of course, was the unstated agreement that we would avoid each other as much as possible. There were the occasional parental-type questions—like now—but that was just for form's sake. As long as there were no arguments or calls from the police station, I knew I could do what I wanted.

"You woke the girls, too. And *they* had to get up for school in the morning."

I scraped the bottom of the carton. "I'm sorry. I'll try to be even more considerate next time."

"Why not just stay out till morning? If you're at a friend's place, sleep there." She ground out her cigarette in the ashtray. "Or you can always sleep in your car."

"It's winter, Mom. It's cold."

"So get your sleeping bag out of the attic. You used to like to go camping. It's the same thing. Probably even better."

I rinsed out the empty carton. "I'm thinking maybe I might move to Florida."

She stopped and looked at me. *"Florida?"*

Hearing the word made me wonder too, but I kept it going. "Yeah. That's sorta what I'm thinking."

"Oh, *really?*" she said, the same voice she would've used if I said I was going to Harvard. "Why Florida?"

"It's where Karla went," I said. "I can stay with some of her friends until I get my own place."

"And what are you going to do for money?"

"Karla works at the Del Mar Hotel and says she can get me a job. I could always work at a mini-mart. I have the experience."

She swirled the cold coffee in her mug, watching it lap close to the brim. "So when are you thinking of doing this?"

Three hundred dollars a delivery, two or three deliveries a week, plus what I made at the Stop-N-Go, minus gas and expenses. If my luck held, we'd have enough money to leave by the middle of the month. And if my luck didn't hold, I'd have a whole other set of things to worry about. "Two weeks," I said. "Three, tops."

"What about school?"

We both knew the answer to that. I was seventeen, and legally I could sign myself out anytime. Or simply stop going. That's what my sister had done, and the world didn't end. But I had a better answer.

"Karla's enrolled in a night school program. I'll sign up for the same thing. We'll study together. We'll have our GEDs by July."

It didn't matter that I made it all up—it was what she

wanted to hear, especially the part about studying with Karla. She kept her eyes on the swirling coffee. "Sounds like you're set on going."

Was I? Even then I didn't know for sure what I was going to do. But I nodded anyway. "Yeah. I am."

After a few dead-quiet moments, my mother sighed and tapped another Winston out of the pack, lighting it with the BIC she kept on the table. "We'll see."

THE PHONE WAS ringing when I stepped out of the shower. No one picked it up, so that meant my mother and sister had left. I got to the phone just as the answering machine clicked on. I shouted a hello over my father's monotone message.

After the beep, Zod said, "You know the Peppermill?"

Of course I knew the Peppermill. Open all night, free coffee refills, and killer pancakes. I'd been there a hundred times.

And yesterday morning, with Dawn.

An hour later I was there again, sitting across from Zod at the back of the empty smoking section, sipping a Pepsi and waiting on a cheeseburger.

Zod flicked open a Zippo lighter and fired up a Marlboro. "Any problems last night?"

Well, there was that gut-punching panic when I thought I was getting pulled over, almost getting ripped off by a fat hillbilly, the long ride home made longer by the old Genesis eight-track I had put in to calm my nerves, and then the cold wait on the dark porch with a bag-load of money as Reg took his time to let me in, but I didn't feel like getting into details. "No. No problems."

"Reg told me about the envelope. That was genius."

"Thanks."

"Seriously, dude. If Fat Sal would have shorted you, you would have gotten the blame. You know that, right?"

"I figured as much."

"How much did Reg pay you?"

I took a sip of my Pepsi and thought fast. Was he looking for a cut? A commission for getting me the job? Maybe that was his angle, the reason he tracked me down in the first place. Maybe he was just curious. Or maybe he already knew. I went with the truth.

"I got three hundred," I said.

His eyes went wide. "That it?"

"Yeah, just that."

He shook his head as he looked at the ceiling. "No, no, no. That's bullshit."

"Honest," I said. "That's all he—"

"That cheap bastard. Three hundred? That's bogus, dude."

Three hundred dollars was more money than I had ever had at one time in my life. It would have taken me weeks to earn it at the Stop-N-Go, yet I made it in less time than I worked on a Friday night. It had seemed like a lot of money for nothing. Now I wasn't so sure.

"You got any clue how much cash you had in that envelope?"

I shrugged. "A couple thousand?"

He laughed, then dropped his voice to a whisper. "Dude, you delivered a *cutie.* A quarter-frickin'-kilo."

I shrugged again.

He leaned in. "There was twenty-two thousand in that envelope."

I heard the number, and for a second it didn't mean anything. Then the math part of my brain kicked in.

Twenty-two thousand dollars.

A new Camaro went for five grand.

My father made sixteen thousand a year at the factory.

In '62, my parents had paid nineteen thousand for our house.

Twenty-two thousand dollars.

And it all fit in an oversize envelope that I had tossed on the floor of my car.

"Reg screwed you over," he said. "He should have given you at *least* five hundred. You need to go back there and tell him you want more."

I thought it through. "No," I said. "I told him I'd do it

for three hundred, and that's what he paid me. If I wanted more, I should have asked for it then."

"You took all the risk."

"I knew that going in."

"The higher-highers gave him three grand for that sale, you know that?"

"Oh, well. That's business."

He stared at me, a smile slowly growing. "I was right about you, dude."

"What's that supposed to mean?"

"I told Reg you were the real deal. Somebody he could trust. Smart, too. Plus, you got balls. But I told you that already. We go way back, dude, you know that?" He set his cigarette in the ashtray.

The way he moved, glancing around the room? Something was up.

"You got this coming," he said as he reached behind his back, and in one quick move, he pulled out his wallet, reached over, and dropped a stack of twenties on my lap.

"You made me look good," he said, taking up his cigarette. "I owe ya."

I FOUND THE book in the exact same place it was last time I was at the public library. Not a lot of people checking out *The Warlord of Bimskala*.

My plan was to crash in the overstuffed chair over by the science books, kill a couple hours before I went back to the Peppermill to meet up with Dawn, but there was an old guy sleeping in that chair, so I settled for the window seat in the reference section that looked out to the parking lot. It wasn't as comfortable and I could feel a draft, but the light was good and nobody came to this part of the library.

I flipped deep into the book, skimming for the big battle scene and the daring rescue of the black-haired princess. It was my favorite part, the one that always transported me to the far-off planet, putting the sword in my hand and the princess in my bed. I read the familiar words, waiting for them to work their magic and pull me in, but after five pages, nothing. Swords still slashed and heads still rolled in the Bimskalan dust, but somehow it wasn't the same. The dialogue was way over the top and the whole plot was silly. Even the princess, with her "heaving bosoms" and "quivering thighs," seemed ridiculous.

I looked at the cover. It was the same drawing that was on the paperback — sexy princess, paper-clip-thin straps on the metal bikini, lots of skin, lusty expression — but it was just a drawing.

It wasn't working.

Dawn, standing at the foot of the bed, wearing a Cheap Trick T-shirt and skimpy red underwear?

Now that worked.

As for the warlord?

You didn't need a sword to be somebody's hero.

I thumbed the pages one last time, then closed the book.

WE SAT IN Dawn's car in the lot near the picnic pavilions at a park, five miles from the Peppermill. I would have been happy staying at the restaurant, but Dawn thought it was too coincidental that Steve—and it was Steve now, "No more of that stupid Zod stuff," she'd said—had picked the same place earlier in the day.

The access roads through the woods were plowed, but it was cold, with a bitter wind. Ours were the only cars around. With the heat cranked, it was toasty warm in her little VW, and the drive-thru coffee steamed up the windows.

"If I had known it was going to be that much cocaine, I would have never let you do it."

I eased the lid off my paper cup and balanced it on the narrow dashboard. "I don't think the amount makes that much difference. Over a couple ounces it's more or less all the same."

"Crime-wise, yeah," Dawn said. "It's the people that get all crazy. You can't trust them as it is. With that much coke on the table, forget it. That's why I made you get the envelope. If they're gonna rip someone off, at least make it a *little* harder."

"I guess if they wanted it that bad, they could have just taken it from me."

"No," Dawn said. "If Reg thought it was them, he'd come looking for them. He may have slipped a bit with his brain half-fried, but he's still dangerous." She tapped another sugar into her cup. "Just ask Freddie."

Neither Reg nor Steve had mentioned Freddie, and I hadn't seen any hint of him at Reg's place. Not like they would put up a "Freddie's body is in the basement" sign.

"The guy in Lockport knows he can't rip off Reg," Dawn said. "Now, framing *you* for it? That he could do. And he tried it, too. He probably would have shorted you just enough to make it look suspicious. Reg has been doing business with him for years, so he'd give the guy the benefit of the doubt. Maybe. Like I said, you never know, when that much coke is involved."

"So in a way, that envelope saved my life."

Dawn shuddered. "Don't put it like that. I hate that you're doing it as it is."

"If you can think of a better way to get the money . . ."

"I know. It's just you're the one taking all the risk, doing this for me—"

"I'm doing it for us," I said, and it felt good saying it.

Right then I should have told her what it all meant to me, how it wasn't just about moving to Florida but moving on with my life, becoming the guy I was pretending to be, and how I was more afraid of failing at that than anything Reg would ask me to do. But before I could say any of it, she said, "You know I can't go without my sister."

I'll be honest. I was hoping she would have forgotten that part.

It was going to be hard enough getting the two of us to Florida. Having a kid in the back seat would only make us stand out more. And I know I'm going to sound like a total asshole, but the truth is, I didn't know a lot of mentally retarded people — not personally anyway — and the idea of driving a thousand miles with her sister made me nervous. What if Terri needed medications or wandered off or freaked out in the car? I know — total asshole — and I felt like a dick even thinking it. Still . . .

"What about your mother? She gonna let you take your sister away?"

Dawn smiled and shook her head. "Trust me, it'll be better for everyone. Especially Terri."

"We can go first, then after we get settled, we can —"

"Absolutely not," she said, and that ended it. "If I go, my sister's going with me."

I sighed to myself. So this is what standing by felt like. "Okay," I said. "If that's the way it's gotta be."

She turned in her seat and looked at me, her eyes holding

on to mine, a lone tear rolling down the curve of her cheek. "Yeah," she said. "That's the way it's gotta be."

I SAT ON the cot in the basement and ran a yellow highlighter down through New York and into Pennsylvania, following the highway until it broke up into smaller state and county roads, somewhere north of Williamsport. I'd found the map in the glove box of my car, along with one of Karla's fake IDs. The map was old and folded all wrong, and only went as far south as North Carolina. We'd need a better one when we hit the road.

And where *was* Venice? I knew it was in Florida and that it was near the ocean, but that was it. Was it on the right side or the left side, up near Georgia or down at the tip? Here I was, telling Dawn how we could get a fresh start in Venice, and I probably couldn't even find it on a map. I made a mental note to snag the road atlas out of the family wagon.

I was staring at the hair-thin lines on the map when I heard the doorbell ring, my nieces racing to open it, some mumbled voices, some laughing, footsteps crossing the kitchen, the door to the basement open, and Steve's voice saying, "Hey, Nick."

I kept it cool. Or tried to, anyway. I put the cap on the highlighter and, without looking, folded the map and tossed it on the floor behind me. Steve didn't seem to notice as he hopped up to sit on the washing machine, swinging a green gym bag onto the dryer next to him. He might have been just Steve, but as he sat there in the basement, I realized that in many ways, he would always be Zod.

"Damn. Living in your parents' basement," Steve said. "That's gotta suck."

"Just for a couple weeks." I didn't want to give anything away, so I added, "My sister's moving out. I'll get my own room back."

"You're making decent money now. You should get your own place."

"Maybe."

"What are you doing tomorrow?"

"I got school in the morning, then nothing much. Why?"

Steve leaned forward, resting his elbows on his knees. "I need some packages delivered."

I felt my stomach start its familiar roll.

"I'd do it myself," Steve said, "but I got bigger things to take care of. It'll take a couple hours, tops. I'll give you eighty bucks."

It wasn't much money, but it would put me that much closer to getting Dawn out of there. "Is this for Reg?"

"No, this is my stuff. Just weed. Too small for Reg to bother with. Eighty is generous. And you're the only guy I trust."

I could picture Freddie and his wispy attempt at a mustache. There was no reason for me to know his name or what he did. And no reason for me to know that Freddie was dead. Only I did know. And I knew it would be stupid to say more, but I wanted to see the reaction, so I asked, "Doesn't Freddie take care of that kind of stuff?"

Steve licked his lips, looked up at the wooden joists of the kitchen floor above his head. "Yeah. But he's . . . uh . . . he's out of town. On vacation."

"Vacation? Must be nice."

"Yeah," Steve said, still looking away, rubbing his hands on his knees.

"Where'd he go?"

"I don't know. Miami, maybe. What the hell do you care?"

"Just curious."

"Well, don't be." Steve slid off the washing machine and tossed the green bag on the end of the cot. "The addresses are inside. It's all paid for, so you won't need your fancy little envelopes. Don't screw it up." He took his car keys out of his coat pocket and headed for the stairs. "Oh. One more thing. Reg needs you on Thursday. You're driving to Watertown. Be there at noon. Don't be late."

"Wait a second." I stood and lifted the bag off the cot. "I didn't say I was going to do it."

Steve kept walking, smiling as he glanced back. "Do you really have a choice?"

WEDNESDAY, JANUARY 4

I PULLED UP TO THE FOUR-WAY STOP SIGN AND TRIED TO remember if the woman at the gas station had said to take a left or a right onto Butterscotch Terrace.

The first two deliveries had been easy. They were on the west side, and I knew the neighborhoods if not the streets themselves. I'd gotten to the first house at eight a.m. If I had gone to school like I was supposed to, it would still be first period, but since I was skipping all that, I was right on time to make the delivery. I knocked, the door opened, I handed over the package, the door closed, and that was it. The second stop was in an apartment complex where every building looked the same. The note in the gym bag had said to look for the apartment with an American flag as a curtain. The guys there invited me in to sample the goods and seemed disappointed when I declined.

The third stop was an east-side address, and that's when things got confusing.

I could count on one hand the number of times I'd been out that way. And it was always as a passenger, never driving. To make it harder, the roads on the east side all had stupid names: Old Walnut Grove Way, Bubbling Creek Trail, Daisy Flour Mill Run, Bridal Path Mews. The more stupid the street name, the more expensive the houses.

After coming to a long and complete stop, I remembered what the woman at the gas station had said, flicked the directional, and turned right, driving past the fieldstone wall, past the gated driveways. Just before the entrance to the country club, I saw the street I was looking for.

Blue Jay Nook Vista Crescent.

There were only four houses on the street, each with a yard big enough to land a plane if it weren't for all the trees. I pulled up the first driveway, following the squared-off hedges around the bend to the covered porch. The front door was six feet wide and painted a rusty red. I was tempted to use the plate-size brass knocker but settled for pushing the doorbell. Inside, a chorus of chimes rolled on and on, playing long after Frank Camden had opened the door.

At first, Frank didn't recognize me, which made sense, since the only place he'd ever seen me was behind the counter at the Stop-N-Go. Sure, he saw me at the frat party too, but that was Drunk Nick, and over the years I'd seen enough beer-soaked Polaroids of myself to know I looked a lot different sober. Frank stood there—one hand on the doorknob, one hand on his hip—his eyes darting as he tried to place the face and the dumpy car. I waited for the light to click on behind his eyes, and when it did, Frank smiled a bright, white, Hently Private School smile.

"Come on in." Frank pushed the door open. "It's Mike, right?"

"Thanks," I said, not bothering to correct him. "I would have been here on time, but I guess I got lost."

Frank pressed the tiny button on the side of his Texas Instruments digital watch. "My mom's gonna be home in few, but we got time." He led the way into the house, cutting through a TV-less living room, around a formal dining table, and into a wood-paneled family room, showing it off without saying a word. The Christmas tree was still up—artificial, silver and blue—and three fluffy stockings still hung above the massive fireplace. Frank sat on the edge of the leather couch, motioning for me to take the recliner. I set the gym bag on the coffee table between us.

"So you're working for our buddy Zod now, huh?"

I smiled to myself at that. "I'm just dropping this off, that's all." I unzipped the bag and handed Frank the package.

Frank held it in his hand. "Anybody but Zod, and I'd weigh this. He's never screwed me over. But there's always a first time, right?"

"Probably."

Frank froze. "Whoa, dude. I'm only joking." He forced a laugh. "Don't go telling him I said that."

I zipped up the bag.

"Seriously," Frank said. "Don't tell him I said that, okay? He can be a little, you know . . ."

"Yeah," I said. "I know."

"Zod's cool, though," Frank said, everything sounding forced now. "Real cool. Like cool on a whole other level."

"Sure."

"Hey, how about that Camaro he drives, huh? You been in that thing? Is that thing bitchin' or what?"

I thought about my rides in Steve's devil-red Camaro, the places it had taken me. "It's something else."

"Hell, yeah." Another nervous laugh. "Hey, he still with that super-hot chick?"

Given Steve's charming personality and goonish looks, I couldn't picture him with a girlfriend. Hookers, yes, but not a girlfriend. "I haven't seen her."

"Damn, bro, she's hot. Nice bod, dark eyes, almost as tough as him."

"Uh-huh." I grabbed the straps of the gym bag. "Like I said, I haven't—"

"Blackest hair I've ever seen on a white chick. Wears it real short."

I paused.

"Don't get me wrong," Frank said, stumbling over his words. "It looks good on her. A little punky, but—"

"Punky, huh?" I took my time, pulling the bag onto my lap as I listened.

"Yeah, you know. Like that chick who plays guitar with the Runaways. Not Lita Ford, the other one."

"Joan Jett?"

"Yeah, that's it," Frank said, snapping his fingers. "Zod's girl looks like that."

I kept my eyes on the gym bag. "Do you know her name?"

"No, but—"

"And you're sure they're together?"

Frank shrugged and tried to smile. He checked the digital display for the time. "So, uh, anyway, my mom's gonna be home soon . . ."

It could be a coincidence.

It wasn't like she was the only one in the world with dark eyes and short, black hair who was smart and tough.

So yeah, it could all be a coincidence.

Or it could be something else.

I slung the bag over my shoulder. It was lighter now, one delivery left to go, back over on the west side.

I'd have a lot to think about on the ride.

FORTY MINUTES LATER, I pulled up in front of the last house on the list.

I didn't need directions. I'd been there before.

There was a doorbell, but I knew that it didn't work, so I pulled open the screen door and knocked. It was a school day, but he was expecting the delivery, so he'd be home, and I could hear the stereo, Boston's "Long Time" cranked loud. I knocked again, harder this time, then the door flew open. Jay glared at me and said, "What do *you* want?"

I hefted the gym bag. "I got a delivery from Steve."

"*Who?*"

I sighed. "It's from Zod."

Jay smirked. "*You* work for the Zod?"

"No, I'm just dropping this off for him," I said. I could have left it at that, but for some reason I wanted to say more. "I work for Reg."

Jay's eyes went wide, his mouth dropped open. I guess it was the reaction I was hoping for. I jiggled the bag. "You want this or not?"

Jay blinked. "Oh, shit, yeah. Sorry. Come on in."

Inside, nothing had changed. I would have been surprised if it had. I'd been hanging out at Jay's house since tenth grade, and other than the occasional holiday decoration, it always looked the same. The furniture never moved. The walls got repainted the same colors. Jay's baby pictures stayed in the frames on the shelf. It should have felt familiar.

Jay turned down the stereo. "So where's Freddie?"

Dead, I thought, but I stuck to the lie I'd been told.

"Vacation." I unzipped the gym bag and tossed the package to Jay. There was nothing left to say, so I turned to leave.

"You hear what happened to Sperbs?"

I shook my head. The last time I had heard about any of them was when Geralyn had dropped by the Stop-N-Go to say how much they all hated me.

"He was at Cici's, up in her room. You been there, right?"

I nodded. Everybody had been there.

"They were getting busy," Jay said, "and her frickin' *dad* walks in."

We both laughed at that—it *was* funny—and for a moment it was like it used to be, like it had been for years, like it could be forever.

"I gotta get going," I said.

Out by the car, Jay said, "If you're not doing anything Friday night, stop by."

I looked back at Jay, at the house, at the room where I had spent a thousand hours, at the life I had left behind. "I'm kinda busy," I said, then—who knows why—I said, "But I'll think about it."

THERE WERE DAYS when I got lucky and had the house to myself.

This wasn't one of them.

When I came around the corner and saw my sister's

rusted Nova and my father's Chevy Caprice Estate station wagon in the driveway, I was tempted to keep going, but I pulled in anyway, too hungry to care.

After my deliveries, I'd wandered the mall for a couple hours, stopping every lap at the same row of pay phones to dial the number Dawn had given Penelope at the Stop-N-Go. I'd let it ring ten, fifteen times, then I'd walk around some more before trying it again. If Reg or one of his crew had answered, I would have hung up, but it just rang.

But even if Dawn had answered, I wasn't sure what I would have said.

I knew it shouldn't have bothered me that she might have been seeing Steve before she moved in with Reg. That was all in the past. Or it would be when we moved. And besides, I had hardly led a virginal life myself. So what if she had slept around a bit? She was going to be with me now, and that was all that mattered.

Or it was supposed to, anyway.

I came in through the garage entrance to the sound of my nieces shouting that they hate—*hate*—beef stroganoff, a dish I had watched them devour many times before. I kicked off my boots and hung my coat on the back of the door, took a deep breath, and braced myself before walking into the kitchen.

My mother spotted me first. "Oh, *now* you show up. Get a chair from the family room. Here, move this. Scoot the girls over. Just do it, please. We have to make room for your *brother.*"

I would have preferred eating in front of the TV, but I knew how that would go over, so I wrestled a folding chair from behind the couch and sat at the table between my father and my sister.

"Get a plate," my mother said. "I'm not your maid."

I stood up, got a plate, a fork, and a glass and sat back down.

My father looked over to the clock on the stove. "He shouldn't get anything. He knows what time dinner is."

I knew. And I was still ten minutes early. But my mom made killer stroganoff, so I kept my defense simple. "Sorry."

My sister passed me a dish of noodles. "Don't take a lot," she said. "It's the only thing the girls will eat."

I leaned forward and smiled down at my nieces—both with mounds of noodles on their plates—before serving myself a child-size portion. I waited until everyone had a chance at the stroganoff before ladling some onto my plate, passing on the steamed carrots but taking extra slices of bread.

For a few minutes it was quiet, everyone busy eating.

It didn't last long.

Jodi declared that she *hated* these *stupid noodles* and wanted *Grandma* to make her *real pasghetti,* and Connie announced that she was *full* and insisted that *Grandpa* take her outside, my mom saying it would only take a couple minutes to boil the water, and my dad telling Connie to get her boots on. Next it was Eileen's turn, telling our mother to stop pampering the girls, shouting to Connie to sit back down this instant and finish eating, the grandparents exchanging eye-rolling glances. It took a minute for everything to settle to a familiar, uncomfortable silence.

Then they remembered I was there.

"You better not have parked behind me," Eileen said. "I have to do some shopping, and I don't want to have to be waiting on you to move your car."

"It's not just your car that needs to move," my mother said, pointing her fork at me as she spoke. "You can't be living in the basement forever. It's not healthy. You need to get with some of your friends and start looking for an apartment now if you plan on moving out after graduation. Unless of course you'd rather pay rent . . ."

Clearly she'd forgotten what I'd said about moving to Florida. Or she knew me better than I thought I knew myself.

"Graduation," my father said, spitting the word out. He reached over to the counter and picked an open envelope out of the stack of mail, dropping it next to my plate. It had the school district logo in the corner, and across the entire front, in blocky capital letters, my father had added a wise and helpful piece of parental advice.

SHAPE UP, MISTER.

I folded the envelope and stuffed it in my back pocket. It wouldn't say anything different than the last letter. I focused on eating before I lost my appetite.

"I'm sick and tired of this," my father said between mouthfuls. "You're going to be eighteen in June."

April.

My sister said, "I was pregnant with Connie, and *I* still managed to finish high school."

Yes, and you've done sooo *much since then.*

"Your father and I *both* had jobs and we *both* graduated on the Honor Roll."

And you both *bring it up every chance you get.*

"You can bet that *his* father never got a letter from the school saying that *his* son was failing two classes."

Just two? I was doing better than I thought.

Then it was my father's turn again. "It's time for you to buckle down, mister. Start acting your age. As long as you're living under my roof . . ."

You'll follow my rules.

". . . you'll follow my rules."

I nodded.

As long as I'm living under your roof.

I CAME IN from moving the cars around. It was tight, but I managed to fit all three vehicles side by side in the driveway.

Now no one was behind anybody else. I knew my sister wasn't going anywhere, but this way she'd have one less thing to bitch about.

My father was alone in the kitchen, staring at his watch when the phone rang. He snapped it up and said hello like normal, then, in a voice loud enough to be heard anywhere in the house, he said, "*A problem with the main assembly line?* Uh-huh. What do the gauges read? Yeah, *ha-ha-ha,* that sounds serious. Oh, I *know* how to fix it. Ha-ha-ha." He hung up the phone, then walked over to the sink and lit a cigarette. After a long, dramatic sigh, he announced, "Looks like I have to go in to work tonight."

"Again?" my mother said, still in front of the TV in the family room. "Can't somebody else do it?"

"Not like me," my father said, taking a drag of his Marlboro, letting it out slow, the dirty grin on his face reflected in the dark kitchen window.

His house, his rules.

Another reason I needed to get the hell out.

AN HOUR LATER I was in the basement, lying on my cot, trying to convince myself we could make it to Florida, that it was even a good idea to try, when the phone rang. My sister answered it, then stomped on the floor, signaling it was for me.

"I hope you don't mind me calling you like this," Dawn said.

"No, it's cool," I said. "I just didn't know you had my number."

There was a pause, then Dawn said, "I found it on Reg's dresser."

"I didn't think he had it, either."

Another pause. "I guess he got it from Steve."

"Yeah, I guess so," I said.

"Can you meet me someplace?"

"What's up?"

"I don't want to talk about it over the phone," she said.

"When?"

"Now. Tomorrow will be too late."

I glanced over at the clock, as if I had something else to do. "Okay. Where?"

She told me. And just like that, the things I'd been lying in my bed thinking about—the questions I was going to ask, the coincidences I needed her to explain—no longer seemed important, that part of my brain shutting down, other parts taking over.

I said, "I'll be right there."

IT WAS SNOWING again, the fat, fluffy kind of flakes that glowed in the headlights and raced into the windshield like the *Millennium Falcon* jumping into hyperspace. It was the kind of snow that made the night darker, and when it covered the road, it could hide long patches of black ice. I drove slower than normal, with the stereo off and both hands on the wheel. There were enough distractions already.

The lot hadn't been plowed yet, but the snow wasn't deep, so I pulled in, parked, and walked up to the door. There was a light on and it was quiet inside. I knocked twice and waited. The curtain moved. I heard the lock turn, then the door opened and Dawn stepped back to let me in.

It was the same room as before, except this time there were no balloons or champagne, no HAPPY NEW YEAR! sign above the TV, just faded wallpaper, mismatched furniture, a couple of lumpy pillows, and tissue-thin sheets on a king-size bed that sagged in the middle. It was small and shabby, and smelled of cigarettes and cheap perfume. There was no pretending what went on in the room. It's what the Wishing Well Motel was there for. I hadn't noticed any of it last time. Not that it would have made a difference. But I noticed it all now. And it still didn't matter, not with Dawn pressing her mouth against mine, her arms wrapped around my neck. A moment later, she said, "Listen. Did Reg give you any new runs?"

"I got one tomorrow. Up to Watertown. We're supposed to get hit with some snow, but it'll all be okay."

"What about next week? Tuesday? Did he say anything about that?"

"No, why?"

She held me tight against her. I could feel her warm body tremble through my winter coat. "You gotta quit. Right now. No more runs. Promise me."

"We don't have enough money yet," I said. "A few more weeks—"

"No! You gotta quit. And we've gotta leave. Now."

"Just tell me why, and we'll—"

"Because I finally figured it out." She took a choppy breath. "I know what Steve's up to."

At that name, you'd think my brain would flick on and take control, dropping out of arousal mode. But no, the focus stayed on the basics—the princess in my arms and the sleazy motel room we were standing in.

Then I saw the look in her eyes. "All right," I said, sitting on the edge of the bed. "What's going on?"

She double-checked the lock on the door as I took off my coat and boots, then she sat next to me, rubbing her hands on her thighs as she spoke. "Steve's setting you up."

That got my attention.

"I wasn't sure at first," she said. "But now I'm positive."

"Setting me up for what? To get busted?"

"By the cops? God, no. He's gonna make it look like it was you."

"*What* was me?"

She swallowed, wet her lips. "Steve is planning to rip off Reg, but he's gonna make it look like you did it."

"Did he *tell* you this?"

"Of course not," she said. "I heard him talking, that's all."

"When?"

"Today." She shrugged. "Some of it before. I don't know. I'm just putting it—"

"What'd you mean you *don't know?*" I stood and started pacing in the cramped space. "What did he say?"

"Please, Nick, don't shout," she said. "I'm a wreck as it is."

I forced myself to sit, a little distance between us this time.

She looked away. "I gotta have a smoke." She pulled her purse off the nightstand and started rummaging through it, tossing a hairbrush, lip gloss, car keys onto the bed, then digging out a bent cigarette from a deep pocket. She straightened it as best she could, lit it, took a long pull. "It was around noon. I was alone in the house. It's rare, so when it happens I like to turn off the TV and read." Eyes closed, she exhaled. "You know that main hallway that goes down to the kitchen? There's a little room off to the side they store stuff in. Boxes, milk crates with car parts. A motorcycle frame. Anyway, behind all that stuff there's this old wing-back chair. It faces straight out the window. The sun was coming in, and it was warm. I must have dozed off because the next thing I can hear Steve talking on the phone in the kitchen, right across the hall. The back of the chair is to the door, so he didn't know I was in the room. He thinks nobody's home, so he's talking normal, but the *way* he's talking—his voice—I could tell something was up."

"Who was he talking to?"

"I don't know. But he described your car, what you look like, the route you'd be on . . ."

"Shit."

"And Steve's saying how he's gonna play it cool, then head to L.A. in June."

"That's stupid. Reg will know he was in on it."

"Maybe," she said. "But Steve's a lot smarter than Reg, which ain't saying much. And Reg is so coked-up all the time anyway. No, he'll convince Reg it was you. He's good like that. Six months from now, Steve will be on his way to California."

"What about the other guys?"

"Lester and Cory? Reg's been sliding. Once this hits, they'll disappear."

"What about me? Won't Reg come looking?"

"He won't find you." Dawn flicked her ash onto the carpet, her hand shaking worse than mine. "No one will. Steve will make sure of that."

The room was too warm, and my head was starting to pound. I was thirsty and sweating, my guts squirming. There was a way out of this, there had to be, but I couldn't get my mind to stop racing to figure out what it was. Dawn finished the cigarette, grinding it into the glass ashtray by the TV, then, feet on the floor, she flopped backwards onto the bed. I joined her, both of us staring up at the mildew stains on the ceiling. We lay there like that for a while, neither of us moving, then I asked, "How's he gonna do it?"

"It doesn't matter. You're gonna quit. We'll leave tomorrow, pick up my sister, and get out of here." She turned her head and looked at me. "Okay?"

I tried to think it through, but nothing would stay still in my head, my fight-or-flight brain taking charge, telling me to get the hell outta there. "All right," I heard myself say, "we go tomorrow."

She reached over and squeezed my hand. Still curious, I said, "How was he gonna do it?"

"There's a run next Tuesday. Reg's been planning it since Thanksgiving. Close to a quarter million dollars."

"Damn."

"It's his comeback deal, him trying to prove that he hasn't lost it yet, that he's still a player. I guess when Steve learned about the money, he started doing some planning, too. He got you in as the runner because he knows you're honest and won't try anything on your own. Then he waited. Tuesday, Reg sends you out to get the money. And you don't come back. Steve would take some heat, and it might get violent, but he'd get away with it."

I counted back the weeks in my head to that day in the Pizza Hut parking lot when Karla said Steve was looking for me. It took him years, but he found a way to get even. "I hate to admit it," I said, "but it's a good plan."

"Yeah, it is." She sighed. "Too bad we didn't think of it."

She said something after that, something about packing light and this brace she had to get for her sister, but the wheels in my head had started turning, so I didn't catch it all.

It took me less than five minutes to get the basic idea down, another five to smooth out the rough spots, then the rest of the night to get Dawn to agree.

THURSDAY, JANUARY 5

IT WAS STILL DARK WHEN I LEFT THE NEXT MORNING. A LOT was going to happen that day, and I needed to start early.

It had snowed a couple inches overnight, the snow falling straight down, so the side windows on my Pinto were clear, but there was enough on the front and back to brush off, so I got to work. It was cold, but the fresh air felt good on my face. I smiled as I thought about the things Dawn and I had gotten around to doing. Then I thought about the things we planned to do today and my smile changed.

My first plan was that we would ride together to Watertown, drop off the coke, pick up the cash, and disappear from there, but Dawn had a better idea. I'd make the run alone, just in case Reg had spotters on the road. She'd go back to Reg's like normal, keep an eye on him, make sure he didn't suspect anything. We'd meet back at the motel room around seven. If it looked good, we'd go, pick up her sister, and head south right then. If not, I'd drop off the cash to Reg, get paid, and we'd leave the next morning.

It was a stupid plan—we agreed on that—but it was the kind of stupid plan that could work.

I brushed off the back window. There'd be no snow to worry about in Florida. I wondered what Karla would say when she saw her old car pull up in front of the Del Mar Hotel. Probably some smartass comment about the way I drove. There'd be questions, too—about Dawn, Terri, the money—and she'd probably be pissed for a few days, but she'd get over it.

I was chipping the ice out from under the wiper blades when I saw the car at the other end of the parking lot. It was ten motel room doors away and covered with snow, but even in the half-light, I knew what it was.

A full-size, luggage-rack-on-the-top, wood-on-the-side, impossible-to-miss 1975 Chevy Caprice Estate station wagon.

I dropped the snow brush and started walking. The closer I got, the more I noticed.

The dent I'd put in the back fender when I was learning to parallel park.

The yellow and black factory parking permit in the side window.

The TAKE THIS JOB AND SHOVE IT! coffee mug sitting on the dash.

On the back seat, the *Sports Illustrated* that had been there since June. On the front, a pair of women's gloves I'd never seen before.

My eyes moved past the windshield, down the long, snow-covered hood of the station wagon, over the guardrail and the walkway to the motel room door.

One kick, and it would fly off its hinges.

One knock, and I'd have my answer.

If I wanted it.

I stood there as long as I could stomach, then I turned and walked away.

I got a dozen steps before I stopped and went back.

I could hear myself breathing, could feel the blood pumping in my fists, my face flushed and hot. I used my hand to brush away the snow, then took the letter from the school district out of my back pocket and wedged it under the driver's side windshield wiper. Even in the darkness, my father's blocky, handwritten words were easy to read.

SHAPE UP, MISTER.

It wasn't enough.

Not even close.

But it would have to do.

I went to my car, started it up, and drove off, no looking back.

BUG-EYED, REG STARED at me across the table. "You ever been to Watertown?"

I shook my head.

"It's three hours in good weather," he said. "It'll be more in this crap. But you leave here, you better get your ass up there and back *to-day*. Understand?"

I nodded.

"I'm dead serious, shithead. I don't care if you have to walk. You make the delivery, and you bring me my money." There was a cigarette burning in the ashtray in front of him, but Reg knocked another from the pack of Kools on the table and lit it, the flame from the lighter flickering with his shaking hand. It took three tries, but he was too coked-up to notice. "I've done the trip in a blizzard. Ten times worse than this. I still made it there and back before midnight."

Steve pulled the tab off a can of Budweiser. "I can go with him."

Reg glared. "Why?"

"Keep him company."

"You're the one who's always telling me how good he is," Reg said, pointing his cigarette at me. "Now you saying he can't do it by himself?"

"He can do it," Steve said. "Just thought he might like the company."

Reg narrowed his eyes. "He don't need *company*. Do you, shithead?"

"No," I said. "I got this."

"*Damn straight* you do," Reg said. He took a drag and

stared at Steve. Steve held the stare for moment, then suddenly got interested in the top of his beer can. Reg turned to me. “This run here today? Eighty grand.”

I felt my eyes go wide, and that made Reg smile.

“You ever seen that much money?”

I shook my head.

“Chump change,” he said. “I’m done with these small-time, nickel-dime deals. Next run you make will be for real money.”

Steve’s lip twitched. A tiny nothing move that sent a chill down my neck.

“Don’t make any plans for Tuesday,” Reg said, then over his shoulder, he yelled, “Hey, babe. Get your ass in here. And bring the bag.”

I heard Dawn shout something back, but the words were lost under a car commercial on the TV. A moment later, a door opened and I caught a glimpse of her coming down the hall. We had agreed, no eye contact, so I kept my head down. I was hoping Reg would ignore me, but when I glanced at him, his eyes were waiting.

“Remember that little talk we had last month? About keeping your mouth shut and how I’d come for you if you tried to dick me over?”

It was three days ago, but I nodded.

“That’s good,” Reg said, shifting his eyes over to Dawn

as she set a gym bag on the table. It was black and gray and brand-new, with the price tag still on the zipper. "Where'd this come from?"

"Where do you think? I bought it," Dawn said, a semi-sweet edge to her voice. "The other one wasn't big enough, remember?"

Reg made a face. "It's the same damn size."

"No," she said, "it's bigger."

It was the same size. There was nothing in our plan about a new bag. It didn't come up at the motel, and if it had, I would have said no, that anything out of the ordinary would only make Reg suspicious. But there it was, out of the ordinary and making Reg suspicious. It was too late to worry about it, so I sat there with my hands in my lap to keep my knees from bouncing.

Reg spun the bag around and opened the zipper. I couldn't see inside, but whatever it was, it made him frown. "I don't like it," he said.

"Well, you put enough of it up your nose," Steve said, smirking as he downed the rest of the can.

"The bag," Reg said. "I don't like it."

Dawn cocked her hips. "Why not?"

"The colors," Reg said. "Too dark."

She laughed.

"I don't find it funny."

"Whatever," Dawn said. "I'll put it in the old one." She reached for the strap, but Reg jerked it away. He hooked a finger in the string loop and snapped off the price tag, zipped the bag shut, and tossed it onto my lap.

Then he did something I didn't expect.

He laughed.

"Have a nice trip, shithead."

I WAS AN hour out of Watertown when the car hit a patch of black ice, swerved hard to the left, whipped back to the right, then went sliding sideways down the road. I pumped the brakes and spun the wheel. Behind me, a semi was coming up quick, blasting its horn, while up ahead, a pair of headlights appeared in my lane. The steering wheel shuddered as the edge of the front wheels caught pavement, then the car spun around, slamming the passenger side into the hard-packed snowbank at the edge of the road.

For a moment I just sat there, shaking too hard to move. The motor was off, but the heater was running on high, the noise of the fan drowning out my gasps. There was a knock on the window and I jumped.

The state trooper smiled. "You all right?"

I rolled down the window. The icy-cold air cleared my head and gave me another reason to shake.

"You handled that well," the trooper said. "Kept your car from bouncing back out in front of that semi."

"Thanks," I said. My voice was high and it broke in the middle of the word, and that made the trooper smile again.

"See if you can get away from the snowbank."

I fumbled for the key, but it wouldn't turn.

"You've got to put it in park first," the trooper said, holding up his hands to stop traffic.

I could feel the eyes of the other drivers on me as I started the car and began to work it loose, inching forward, then backing up, then forward again, then back, then forward, each time a little farther. It felt like it took an hour, but three minutes later the car was free, and I was driving north on the road to Watertown.

The weather wasn't as bad as everybody had been predicting. It was snowing, but it was no blizzard.

I'd just hit a patch of ice.

Could happen to anybody.

And troopers spent half their days in the winter helping drivers out of ditches.

No big deal.

But a state trooper tapping on your window when you had a gym bag full of cocaine in the car, just to compliment you on your driving? That was the kind of luck that could make you sick if you thought about it.

What the hell was I doing?

If I got busted with that coke, that'd be it—I'd be locked up the rest of my life.

Even if the cops pulled me over on the way back, I'd still have to explain where I got all the money. Guys my age had no reason to have that much cash.

Eighty thousand dollars.

Two people could live for years on that, not working, spending every day at the beach.

Or in bed.

But there weren't two people.

There were three.

Me, Dawn, and Terri.

Most of that money might end up going to medical stuff. Dawn had mentioned that Terri needed a brace to ride in the car. What else would we have to buy? Even eighty grand wouldn't hold out forever. Eventually, we'd have to get jobs, our great adventure reduced to a two-bedroom apartment somewhere, our little, strange new family growing old together.

For the rest of the ride, I had one thought: *What the hell am I doing?*

THE MAN OPENED the Chips Ahoy bag and offered it to me before reaching in for a cookie.

He said his name was Diesel. He was old—forty, maybe more—big in that way ex-bodybuilders get, with two chins and a doughy, low-hanging gut that hid his belt. He had a

Montreal Expos mug in his hand and a pistol in his pants pocket.

"I knew Reg wouldn't make the drive up here."

"It's not that bad," I said. "I took Route 11. Some slippery spots, but if you go slow, it's okay."

Diesel bit the cookie in half and washed it down with a swig of coffee. "Not the weather. The cops."

"There were some. But they were busy with accidents. Cars off the road. That kind of thing."

"Exactly," he said, finishing his cookie. "That's why we checked the weather before we green-lighted today. We knew they'd be distracted. Still, not enough for Reg, I guess." He held the bag out again. "You sure you don't want one?"

I shook my head. I hadn't eaten since I'd wolfed an Egg McMuffin for breakfast. I was hungry, but I doubted I could keep anything down.

"Why didn't Reg send the other dude? Short guy, got a little pubic mustache going?"

I could picture him. "Freddie."

"Yeah, that's the dude. Where is he?"

I wished I knew. If I did, Dawn and I could go to the police, and they'd dig up the body or drag the lake or sift a pile of ashes for teeth. It would be the end to Reg and Steve and the others, and the start of us. But I didn't know, so Reg was still there. I said, "I heard he's on vacation."

"Must be nice." He drained the last of his coffee and put his cup in the sink. "Okay, let's see what Reg sent." He unzipped the bag and set two packages on the counter, each one no bigger than a carton of cigarettes, both covered in layers of plastic wrap and cellophane tape. I remembered the way the last delivery went. Dale and the fat man had weighed the package on an electronic scale, then the woman used a small glass of bleach to test the purity before they sampled it for themselves. But this was a lot more coke and a lot more money.

He picked up one of the packages and bounced it in his hand. "Looks good to me. Nice job, kid."

I blinked. "*That's it?* You don't have to check it or anything?"

He raised an eyebrow. "For what?"

"I don't know. Make sure it's all there? That it's pure?"

He laughed. "It's never pure, kid, you ought to know that. And as for weight, Reg wouldn't burn us. He knows better."

Us? I looked around. It was a small house, and the doors to the bathroom and lone bedroom were open. I didn't see anybody else. But I did see the black leather jacket hanging on a hook by the back door. In the center was a flying skull, below that a patch that said Montreal, and at the top, across both shoulders, another patch with two words: HELL'S ANGELS.

"I suppose you want the cash." He bent down, opened a cupboard door, and took out a grocery bag, the top rolled down two-thirds of the way. He flipped the bag over. Dozens of inch-thick stacks spilled onto the counter—tens, twenties, fifties—each stack wrapped with a paper band.

I knew my mouth was hanging open, but—*damn*—that was a *lot* of money.

The man nodded at the tumbled-down pile. "You want to count it?"

It took a few seconds for the words to register. "No," I said. "Looks good to me."

The man laughed. "Good answer, kid." He swept the stacks into the new black and gray bag, jostling them around till they all fit, then hung the strap on my arm. "You see the cash in there? Good. Now you close it. And don't let that bag outta your sight for a second."

I zipped the bag shut and moved the strap onto my shoulder.

Diesel put the bricks of coke in the A&P bag, rolled the top down like before, and placed it in the cupboard over the counter. "Can I get you a sandwich or something? There's some orange juice in the fridge if you'd like."

"Thanks," I said, "but I gotta get going. Reg is expecting me back on time, and I don't want to get stuck in the snow or anything."

The man stopped, then looked hard at me. "Hold on." He pointed at the table as he crossed room. "Take a seat. I wanna make a call."

"I was kinda hoping to—"

"Sit," the man said.

I sat.

The man took the receiver off the phone and punched in a number. I heard him say hello, say some things about the roads and traffic, heard myself described as "some kid," heard him joke about my shirt and tie, heard part of a mumbled comment about taking a drive, then I heard the man hang up, the whole time just wanting to get out of there. I may have been just "some kid," but I was smart enough to know that when a Hell's Angel with a pistol in his pocket tells you to sit, you stay sitting.

The man strolled to the counter and picked up the Chips Ahoy bag. "I called a friend of mine about you," he said.

I looked up.

"Told him I didn't like it," the man said. "Told him to get over here."

I could feel the sweat start to bubble up on my lip. "Look, I don't want any—"

"What, you thought I was just gonna let you go?"

I paused, then nodded.

"Ain't happening, kid," the man said.

"But I have—"

"But nothing," the man said. "You ain't going anywhere till Wally gets here."

I tried to swallow.

The man fished out another chocolate chip cookie and held it up as he talked. "Wally drives a snowplow for the town. He'll lead the way as far south as the county line. After that, just drive slow. I don't wanna see you get hurt."

IT WAS TEN THIRTY when I pulled into the parking lot of the Wishing Well Motel. It would have been an hour earlier, but I had to wait for Wally, then follow behind his slow-moving plow for forty miles. Every minute counted now, and the sooner Dawn and I were on the road, the farther away we'd be when Reg realized what had happened.

There weren't many cars in the lot—and no full-size, luggage-rack-on-the-top, wood-on-the-side station wagons—so I was able to park in front of our room. I saw the curtain in our window move, and as I climbed out of the car, the motel room door flew open and Dawn ran to me, her arms wrapping around my neck.

"Oh my god, you're safe," she said. "I've been so worried, looking out the window every two seconds, wondering where you were . . . I'd hear an ambulance go by or *something,* I don't know . . . and then a car would pull up and it . . . it . . . wasn't you, and . . . and . . ."

For a perfect moment we stood there, holding on to each

other, the light from the room spilling out around us as a fresh layer of snow began to fall. Then a loud truck drove past on the road above, and Dawn gasped and pushed away, her eyes wide. She took my arm and pulled me in the room, double locking the door and leaning to look through the peephole.

I glanced around the room.

The bed was made, but it was covered in cut-up newspapers and magazines, a pair of scissors on top of a *Cosmo.* There was an empty take-out container in the trash, and on the nightstand, an ashtray full of cigarette butts, a crumpled pack of Virginia Slims, a packet of soy sauce, and a pile of rubber bands.

I tossed the bag on the bed. Dawn turned slowly and looked at the bag. Then she looked at me. "No. Don't put it there." She took the bag, dropped to her knees, and stuffed it under the bed. She stumbled as she stood and I caught hold of her, her whole body shaking. "Sorry," she said. "What if somebody sees it?"

"Nobody's gonna—"

"I know, Nick. I'm sorry. I'm just really scared."

I held her, hugging her body tight against mine, one hand around her waist, the other stroking the back of her neck. She took a deep breath and looked at me, the dark sparkle returning to her eyes. She reached up and touched my cheek. We kissed, soft at first, then long and hard, and it would have led to more if I'd let it.

"We gotta go," I whispered.

I could feel her head shake against my shoulder.

"We can take turns driving," I said. "We can make it to Virginia by morning."

"No."

"Sure we can. Come on. We gotta get outta town now. When I don't show at Reg's, they'll start looking for my car. If they find us here . . ."

"He's not going to look for us," Dawn said.

I laughed.

"He's not going to care what we do. None of them will," she said, slipping away to sit on the edge of the bed.

Not now, I thought, but I sat next to her anyway, took her hand in mine. "We need to get on the road right away so—"

"No, we don't, Nick. You're not doing this."

"It's done," I said. "I got the money. All we need to do is go, and we're—"

"And we're what? Running for the rest of our lives? Always looking behind us? Jumping every time there's a knock on the door? I don't want to live like that."

"It won't be that bad. You it said yourself. Reg is losing it and Steve's got his own plans."

She sighed. "Don't you get it? Don't you see how we'd be starting off?"

"Yeah. With eighty grand."

"I gotta think of Terri. You have to know that, Nick." She turned to face me. "Remember when we first met?"

"At the Stop-N-Go."

"Do you know what it was that I liked about you?"

"That I let you rip me off?"

She smiled and lowered her head. "You were different. You weren't like the people in my life. You were funny and kind, and—" She laughed. "You were a *good person.* And then you showed up at Reg's, and I thought I'd been wrong. But the more I learned, the more I saw you, the more I knew I'd been right."

"I'm not a saint."

"No, but you're not like them, either. But if you take the money, that's what you'll become. Trust me."

"What about Florida?"

"We'll get there," she said. "Not right now, but soon."

I felt a weight sliding off my back and realized then that, despite what I had said, despite my list, I wasn't ready to leave.

"We have a couple hundred bucks," she said. "And time to save more."

I gestured at the newspapers and magazines. "Is that why you spent the day cutting coupons?"

She glanced at the bed, and for a moment it was if she didn't remember. Then she said, "Yes. Coupons."

"That's not going to save us much."

She squeezed my hand. "It'll get us closer. That's the important thing."

I felt my chest tighten, felt something in my throat. I brushed the hair off my forehead, my fingers rubbing against my eyes. I took a breath and wet my lips. "So what do we do now?"

Dawn bent down and reached under the bed. "Take this to Reg," she said, hanging the bag on my shoulder. "Then come back to me."

I'D DONE IT.

I stood out from the crowd.

I stood up for what mattered.

I stood fast when things got rough.

And I stood by the woman I knew I loved.

I followed my list, and it led me to this moment.

I shifted the bag to my other shoulder and knocked on the door.

I was about to walk into a murdering drug dealer's house to hand over the eighty thousand dollars I'd gotten from a Hell's Angel for delivering a kilo of cocaine, and I couldn't remember a time when I'd been happier.

The door opened and Cory said, "Well, don't just stand there grinning like an idiot. Get in here."

I stepped in and stamped the snow off my boots. Cory relocked the door, mumbling about heating the damn outside, then disappeared down the hall.

The late local news was on the TV, but the sound was drowned out by the funky beat pumping from the stereo. There was a bong on a folding chair by the couch and an empty pizza box on the floor.

Reg and Lester sat at the table, Lester shuffling cards, Reg staring at me.

"You cut it close there, shithead. Another hour, we would have come looking for you."

"The roads were pretty bad around Oswego," I said.

Reg gave a disgusted sigh, crushed his cigarette butt in the ashtray. "I don't know why I hired your sorry ass in the first place."

"Steve," Lester said, still shuffling.

"Oh, that's right," Reg said. "*Steve.* Been after me for *weeks* to give shithead here a shot."

"Longer than that," Lester said.

Reg looked at me. "He must owe you big-time."

I smiled to myself. It was the other way around. If it wasn't for Steve bringing me to Reg's house, Dawn would have simply been this hot chick who once conned me out of ten dollars. Funny how it worked out like that.

"Nicky! My man." The kitchen door swung open and out stepped Steve, smiling like he'd won a quarter-million-dollar bet. He strode over and slapped an arm around my shoulders. "Up to Watertown and back, and it ain't even midnight. I told you Nick was the real deal. I'd stake my life on it, right, Nicky boy?"

"You said that about Dawn, too," Reg said, knocking another cigarette out of the pack. "Then she got sloppy with the accounts, adding wrong, losing money . . ."

Lester gave a half laugh. "Losing it in her purse."

Steve waved a hand, dismissing it all. "That bitch is crazy. Runs in her family. Mom's a junkie, her sister's brain-dead . . ."

"Dawn ain't much better," Reg said. He lit the cigarette, took a long drag. "I swear, she don't give a shit about anybody but that wacked sister."

Reg leaned back and blew a perfect smoke ring.

And as I watched it float to the ceiling, something clicked.

The coincidences that couldn't be chance.

The clues I'd missed.

The one truth I ignored.

I'd do worse things than that for my sister.

My stomach groaned, knowing then what had happened. And sensing what was coming.

Reg snapped his fingers. "Hey, shithead. I'm talking to you. Give me the bag."

I stood there and, for a flash of a second, nothing moved. Then, with an inaudible pop, it started again, everything in slow motion, all sounds merging into a dull, sickening roar.

Reg saying something I couldn't hear.

Lester pushing the cards away, clearing a space.

Steve reaching over, taking the bag off my shoulder, setting it on the table.

The bag that had held a kilo of cocaine.

The bag that the Hell's Angel had filled with money.

The bag that I'd looked in as I drove back home.

The bag that hadn't been out of my sight for a single second.

Until Dawn put it under the bed.

The bed that we'd slept in together the night before.

The bed that, twenty minutes ago, had been covered in bits of paper.

I looked at the bag.

Black and gray.

Exactly the same.

Except this one still had the price tag that I'd seen Reg tear off.

I watched as he pulled the zipper back and dumped out stack after stack of bill-size clippings from newspapers and magazines, each stack wrapped tight with a rubber band.

A FEW DAYS LATER

I PULLED INTO THE EMPTY SPACE, PUT THE CAR IN PARK, AND sat there, trying to make sense of it all.

I should have been dead.

When the stacks hit the table, and it was clear it wasn't money, I figured that was going to be the last thing I ever saw.

Obviously, it wasn't.

What I did see was Reg's coked eyes bug out as he pounded the table with his fist.

I saw Lester pick up a fat stack of newspaper clippings, give it a thumb-through, then toss it back on the pile, not even trying to hide his smirk.

And when I glanced over at Steve, expecting to see a knife, I saw him looking at me, his hand moving slow and just enough for me to notice, palm down and patting the air. If he was trying to tell me not to move, he didn't have to bother. I could barely breathe, let alone run.

Reg swept his arm across the table, sending the stacks flying, then spun around and started pacing the room, kicking in a stereo speaker and hurling the bong at the TV, colored glass and dirty water spraying the wall. Then he ran down the hallway, shouting, swearing, punching the air as he went into one of the bedrooms. Steve turned and put a finger in my face. "Don't say shit." He looked at Lester. "You in?"

Lester paused, then nodded.

There was the muffled sound of something smashing, then Reg stormed back, his arm straight out in front of him, the pistol level with my head as he shouted, "Give it to me!"

Steve had warned me, but I was the one looking down the black hole of the barrel. Before I could say a thing, Reg clocked me on the jaw with the butt of the pistol. I staggered. *"Come on, come on,"* Reg was shouting, "Diesel's address. *Now!*"

My hands moved on their own, digging into the pockets of my jeans, finding the slip of paper.

Reg snapped it out of my hand. "Shithead here's too smart to try to play *me,* ain't that right, shithead?"

I stood there, waiting.

"Problem is, shithead, you're dumb enough to get taken by Diesel." He made a noise like a laugh. "Tell 'em, Steve. *Tell 'em* what I'm gonna do."

Steve said, "He's gonna go up to Watertown and get his money."

"Damn straight. *Nobody* messes with me. I knew I

shouldn't have trusted that fat bastard. But it's cool, man, it's *real* cool—I know where we stand now, him and me. It's all clear. I see it, I see his little punk-ass play." He tossed Steve a set of keys. "Start my car. Lester here's gonna cut me three fat lines. Then I'm gonna go get what's mine."

Steve grabbed a fistful of my sleeve, knocking me off balance. "Let's go, Nicky," he said, and started walking—out the door, down the porch stairs, and into the shadows, shoving me hard up against his Camaro. Through gritted teeth he said, "You stupid, stupid shit."

"I . . . I didn't know . . . I just—"

"Not you, dipshit," he said. "Me."

I turned, ready to fight if I had to. But Steve was smiling.

"I should have figured she was up to something," he said, shaking his head. "Asking too many damn questions, telling Reg what a good little boy you were, buying that bag. I should have figured it out."

I was still struggling with it. "So Dawn . . . she . . . you think . . ."

"Oh, hell yeah. I should have seen it coming. She's been acting weird, all *nice* and *happy*. Been like that for a week. No. Before that." He looked at me. "Since *you've* been around."

"*Me?* Wait. You think that Dawn and I . . ."

He grunted. "You wish." He shook a smoke from a pack of Marlboros, lit it. "Eighty grand. Looks like she's getting outta here after all," he said, and shook his head, his smile growing. "She's something else."

"Yeah, I suppose," I said, not sure how I felt. Or wanted to feel.

"Listen. I've been talking with the higher-highers. From what I've been telling them, they'll assume Reg was trying to rip 'em off. They'll put me in charge. And the first thing they're gonna tell me to do is clean house. The higher-highers know Lester and Cory, so those two are safe." Then he looked at me. "But they don't know you."

He took a drag off his cigarette, the red glow lighting his face. I didn't like where this was going.

"There's two ways I can handle this," he said. "The smart, easy way or the stupid, risky way. The stupid thing would be for me to let you squirm outta this, since you actually ended up doing me a favor. But there'd always be a chance you'd say the wrong thing to the wrong person, and I'd end up paying for it. The smart thing I'm sure you can guess."

I could. It didn't make it any better.

We stood there looking at each other. Then he put Reg's keys in his pocket and gave me a shove toward my car. "If I ever see you again, I *will* do the smart thing. Understand?"

I nodded.

He gave me one last look, then started back for the front door. "Time for you to move on, Nick."

So I did.

» » »

IT TOOK ME a few days, but I got to where I was going.

The sun was just coming up when I pulled into the parking lot. I put my hands on the steering wheel and stretched. A road map on the seat next to me, the Runaways on the radio. And Dawn on my mind.

I suppose I should have hated her. She'd set me up from day one, knowing there was a good chance she was going to get me killed. And she let me waltz into Reg's place with a bag full of cut-up newspapers while she took off with the money.

That was one way of looking at it.

You could also say that she loved her sister, and she wanted a better life for both of them. She just needed the help of a good person to get it. Maybe I didn't get the ending I wanted, but she gave me the start I needed. Because without her, odds are I wouldn't have changed at all.

And that's how I'd always remember her.

I turned off the car and climbed out. It was too warm for a winter coat, but it's all I had, so I put it on over my black T-shirt. My white button-down shirt was in the trunk with my other clothes. The tie was hanging on a road sign, somewhere in West Virginia.

I took out my wallet and checked my finances — eighty-five dollars and whatever change had accumulated in the ashtray. Stuck in between a couple of bills was my list. I took it out, unfolded it, read the words in the dim light.

STAND OUT.
STAND UP.
STAND BY.
STAND FAST.

If only it was that easy.

I folded the list into a tight square, then flicked it away.

Across the street was the Del Mar Hotel and, just past that, the Gulf of Mexico.

A good place to start over.

If it was going to happen — and it *was* happening — it had to start sometime. That morning looked right to me.

ABOUT THE AUTHOR

CHARLES BENOIT's teen novels include *Cold Calls, Fall from Grace,* and *You,* an ALA Quick Pick for Reluctant Young Adult Readers. Charles is a former high school teacher and the Edgar-nominated author of three adult mysteries. A 1977 high school grad, Charles maintains that any resemblance between himself and Nick is not coincidental. On the weekends, he plays tenor sax with Some Ska Band in his hometown of Rochester, New York. Visit him at www.charlesbenoit.com or follow him on Twitter (@BenoitTheWriter).